The Twelfth Town

Three Rivers Ranch Romance™
Book 11

Liz Isaacson

ISBN-13: 978-1-63876-341-3

"For with God nothing shall be impossible."

Luke 1:37

Chapter One

T he long row of cabins at Three Rivers Ranch had never looked more glorious than they did to Taryn Tucker. She stood at the end of them on a Monday morning, her gaze stretching across all twelve of them, the same way she had last week after she'd been offered the job of cleaning them.

Playing maid was a long way from having a professional makeup artist paint her face and a stylist make sure every strand of hair fell the right way. But Taryn much preferred this life to the one she used to have.

Or at least she hoped she would. With eleven small towns behind her, she desperately wanted to find one to live in for a while. She tucked her newly dyed black hair into a ponytail and then stuffed the ends into a messy bun before stooping for her cleaning supplies. Might as well get started.

She thought about the apartment she'd been able to find in Three Rivers, a town she'd stumbled upon quite by accident the week before. She'd never seen quite such an enthusiastic Halloween celebration before. Not even in New Orleans, where she'd been assigned one October a few years ago—and they knew how to celebrate death in Louisiana.

She'd used the last of her meager paycheck from town number eleven, where she'd worked bagging groceries until she got too nervous to stay, to pay for a hotel for a couple of nights until she found the one-bedroom unit above the barber shop on Main Street.

They won't follow you this far, Taryn told herself as she mounted the steps to the first cabin, the one closest to the homestead where she'd been instructed to replenish her cleaning supplies.

At least Taryn hoped they wouldn't. She wasn't even sure who "they" were, only that someone from her former employer wanted to know where she'd disappeared to. As if the public humiliation she'd caused as well as endured couldn't be viewed twenty-four hours a day via the Internet.

Six months had passed. Surely the news station would find another story to focus on, especially in a city the size of Corpus Christi. Taryn had been praying for a hurricane, and though they sat in the thick of the season, God had not granted her requests for such a storm. It was just as well. She didn't want to be responsible for tragedy and death just to get the attention off her messed up personal life.

She mourned the loss of such a life as she fitted the master key into the lock. Still, the owner of the ranch, Squire Ackerman, hadn't seemed to recognize her— *and why would he?* she asked herself.

Corpus Christi television stations didn't broadcast to dinky Three Rivers. But somehow, Taryn carried the weight of who she'd been and it cumbered her shoulders, weighed her down.

She entered the cabin and set her bucket of supplies on the floor so she could return to retrieve the vacuum cleaner. Apparently cleaning the cowboy cabins was a brand-new job; Squire had never hired someone to do it before. According to him, his cowboys right now were of the messy variety.

Taryn lugged the vacuum up the steps and into the cabin, pausing to wipe the first inklings of sweat from her forehead. She clutched the bucket with one hand and towed the vacuum behind her with the other as she headed for the bedroom in the back of the quiet cabin. She'd mapped out a plan of attack to get three of the twelve cabins done each day, and that started with working from the back to the front. Each cabin would be done in two hours, with fifteen-minute breaks in between.

Squire had agreed to her plan during the second interview, and given her the requested four-day work week. Taryn was really looking forward to a three-day weekend each week, and her spirits lifted as she barged through the bedroom door.

"Hey!" A man stood there, barely wearing a pair of jeans. He fumbled with the zipper while Taryn stared. With his pants securely in place, he folded his arms across his bare chest. His impressively wide bare chest.

"Who might you be?" He grinned at her, an action which made her mortification fall down a notch. He reached for a white undershirt lying on the unmade bed and pulled it over his sandy-haired head. He obviously hadn't shaved that morning—or any morning in the past month. Red and lighter brown salted his beard, which he'd trimmed neatly along his jawline.

Taryn swallowed, unable to find her voice. His blue-gray eyes sucked at her. They seemed filled with lightning, with laughter, with life. She envied him immediately.

"It's no big deal," he said. "I just don't normally have pretty women back here." He pulled a blue and black plaid shirt from his closet and put it on. "My name's Kenny Stockton." He stepped toward her and offered his hand.

She dropped her cleaning bucket and put her hand inside his, and it looked child-sized comparatively. She swallowed and took a calming breath. He didn't seem upset she'd walked in on him. "Taryn Tucker." She cringed at her near-perfect delivery, as if she was signing off one of her newscasts. *I'm Taryn Tucker. Good-night, Corpus Christi.*

"Pleased to meet you, Taryn Tucker." He looked at her curiously, but he didn't seem to recognize her. She glanced around for a television in his bedroom and didn't find one. Her muscles softened, and she allowed herself to smile at the handsome cowboy who still held her hand.

"Sorry I barged on in," she said. "I didn't think anyone would be home. Squire said the cowhands are up early to do their jobs."

Kenny slid his hand away from hers. "Yeah, I got real dirty during the haul this mornin'. Came back to shower before heading over to the admin trailer for my next assignment." He glanced around, as if just now noticing that beds could be made. "Sorry about the mess."

She forced herself to give a light giggle. "That's my job. If you go doin' it, I won't get paid." And she needed the money. Her salary had long dried up, and the hourly-wage jobs she'd been getting by with never seemed to pay enough.

At least you're not sleeping in your car, she thought as she searched for an outlet to plug in the vacuum.

That night—though it had only been a single night—had been one of the worst of her life. Worse than the night she'd said no to her boyfriend's proposal on live TV.

A chill ran down her back, and she lifted her hand in acknowledgement when Kenny said he was heading out. Relief spread through her when the front door banged closed behind him, and Taryn sank onto his bed. No tears came—she'd cried them all out in the first three months.

Just pure exhaustion. She needed to get out of Texas if she had any hope of living a normal life. But as it always did, the thought of returning home to South Dakota brought on a wave of nausea Taryn had learned to swallow down and breathe through. Her parents hadn't seen the debacle—she doubted they had any idea that she'd left Corpus Christi six months ago—but she didn't want to return to Bottle Hollow and explain why. After all, she'd vowed never to return when she'd left a decade ago.

She spoke to her mother from time to time, but her father still hadn't opened the lines of communication. Some words took longer to fade to whispers, Taryn supposed. Or perhaps her father was as stubborn as her mother always said he was.

She inhaled deeply to inflate her chest and focused on the closet in front of her. A gray camouflage hint of fabric caught her eye, and she sprang to her feet and shoved the clothes which concealed the uniform to the left.

U.S. Marines.

Her chest rose and fell in shallow breaths. *Stockton* sat above the right breast pocket, and Taryn wondered where he'd been stationed, how he'd gotten out of the Marines, and why he'd chosen ranching instead of something like law enforcement the way her brother had.

She took a deep drag of air, expecting to find the woodsy, spicy scent of Collin. She didn't. She hadn't since his death three years ago. Still, something about this desert cammie called to her.

Another breath revealed a new scent, one that wrapped through her soul and wound around her toes. This one smelled like fresh cotton, and outdoorsy dryer sheets, and something deeply masculine.

Kenny's scent.

Taryn closed her eyes and reveled in it, a fistful of his uniform clutched in her fingers. Something beyond the house snapped, and her eyes snapped open. She stumbled away from his personal belongings. Embarrassment flooded her.

"Get a grip," she muttered to herself as she started the vacuum. She attacked the clutter and dust in Kenny's cabin with vigor. After all, she wasn't in town to get involved with another marine, even if he smelled as wonderful as she imagined heaven to be. Even if his eyes carried a twinkle and his deep voice sang to her soul and his muscles testified of his impressive physique.

No, she'd had enough of cops and servicemen. Enough of watching them die, the way her brother had. Enough of dating them and then humiliating them when they proposed to her.

Familiar remorse combined with an inexplicable rage hit her right behind the breastbone. Chris should've known not to surprise her like that. Nothing about their year-long relationship had suggested she'd enjoy an on-air proposal.

Her refusal *was* his fault, and yet she'd lost everything because of it. Taryn left Kenny's cabin in tip-top shape, determined not to let her ex-boyfriend into her thoughts, her decision-making, her life. Not anymore.

As she entered the next cabin, she looked up into the rafters of the porch as if gazing toward heaven. *Help me find what I need here,* she prayed. If only she knew what that was and how to get it.

"WHAT'S YOUR DEAL TODAY?"

Kenny looked up at Lawrence's question, his mind

still trying to focus on organizing the words into a sentence that made sense. He blinked and looked at the horse he'd been brushing. "No deal."

"I've been talking to you, and you don't respond." Lawrence led his horse into the stall and latched it. "It's like you've got a lot on your mind." He leaned against the fence and grinned. "But you're Kenny, so that can't be true."

Kenny chuckled with his friend. "I suppose I've been distracted today." Distracted by a gorgeous pair of brown eyes and hair he'd been speculating on its true color for most of the day. The black on Taryn obviously came from a bottle.

"You been lookin' at a new horse?"

A twinge of disdain pinched behind Kenny's eyes. But Lawrence wouldn't automatically assume Kenny had been distracted by a woman. He rarely made it past the third date, and the last woman he'd been out with declined his dinner invitation, claiming he was "too happy."

Well, Kenny didn't know how to be unhappy. Didn't really seem to be in his nature, and he certainly wasn't going to apologize about his glass-half-full atti-tude. His time in the Marines had taught him to see the darkness, the evil, the horrors of this world. He didn't want to exist there all the time.

He thanked God everyday that he'd been able to

serve his country without losing his life. So many others didn't. He'd served two four-year terms of active service before leaving the Marines, before wandering the country in search of what to do next, before he'd found Three Rivers Ranch. His father had known Garth Ahlstrom in Montana, and Kenny had come to Texas a few years ago looking for a job. Garth hired him the same day. Another blessing.

"Hello?" Lawrence waved his hand in front of Kenny's eyes. "Must be a beautiful horse."

"Hm." Kenny didn't correct him. So he'd thought Taryn was pretty. Every man who looked at her surely thought that too. She was petite and polite, which led Kenny to believe she'd been raised in the South.

The heat from her hand still burned in his, and he fisted his fingers as he finished his last chore before heading back to his cabin. For one small moment, he fantasized about walking in on Taryn. But the idea was ridiculous. Squire had hired her to clean all the cabins, as well as the administration building. It wouldn't take her all day to clean his cabin, though it was a bit of a pig sty.

Sure enough, when he tried to enter his cabin, the door was locked. He fished his keys from his pocket and entered the quiet cabin. His roommate, Charlie, would be home in a few minutes, and Kenny took the opportunity while he was alone to admire the freshly vacuumed rugs, the straight pillows on the couch, and his crisply made bed.

Kenny wondered where Taryn had come from. He hadn't seen her at church previously, but that was his only interaction with anyone off the ranch. Maybe she didn't go to church. And it wasn't like he went every single week either.

"Wow, this place looks great." Charlie entered the cabin and kicked his dirty boots onto the clean rug. "What're you thinkin' for dinner?"

Kenny hadn't thought of anything but Taryn for hours. He hadn't discovered how to get her number, or what her schedule at the ranch would be, or anything. He didn't want to ask. Didn't want anyone to know of his interest.

The wind shook the windows as Kenny said, "Pizza or spaghetti."

"You cooking?"

"Sure." He stepped into the kitchen and pulled out a stock pot.

"This place smells like lilacs," Charlie commented, and Kenny smiled as he salted the pasta water.

* * *

THE NEXT MORNING, Kenny didn't see Taryn on his way to the administration building. Garth had messaged all the cowhands about a mandatory meeting that morning, instead of just heading out to their usual chores.

"Maybe we'll get our new assignments," Charlie commented.

"Nah." Kenny grinned at him as they climbed the steps to the building. "We just got new ones last month."

"Yeah, you're right." Charlie lowered his head against the wind, his tone resigned. Kenny didn't much care what his chore was, though there were definitely less desirable jobs around the ranch. Kenny was just glad to be out of a uniform, working the hours of the day away, and living a carefree life.

A flash of black hair caught his attention, but he didn't truly have a chance to see if it was Taryn or not before Charlie opened the door and ushered Kenny into the admin building. They took seats and waited for Garth to appear. By the time he finally did, Kenny had listened to Lawrence and Charlie bicker good-naturedly about whose dog was smarter and why.

"Storm comin' in," Garth said as a way to call the cowboys to order. It worked. "I reckon we have today to get the animals secure, get the barns all closed up, and the rest of the week, we'll be working on indoor improvements."

Some of the cowboys shuffled their feet, but not

Kenny. He didn't mind working inside any more than he did outside. Someone asked what kind of indoor improvements, and Garth mentioned painting and appliance repair in some of the cabins, maybe laying new flooring in a couple of them, and other home improvement items Kenny had never done. But he could wipe a brush up and down and follow written directions.

The meeting ended with assignments to get the livestock on the ranch secured, and Kenny got assigned along with a half-dozen cowhands to ride out and check on the herd. They'd hunker down next to the tree line for some security, and Kenny labored with the other men to make the field smaller. Keeping the cattle in a group would help them stay calm, and it was only supposed to rain. Buckets, but just rain.

Kenny drove another nail into the plywood back Garth had instructed they build on the existing roof structure that protected the feeding troughs. The cattle wouldn't be able to access the hay from both sides, but the chances of their feed lasting through the storm increased with the additional wall.

"Roof's secure," Lawrence said from the other side of the structure. "This is almost done."

"Great work," Garth said. "The hay'll be here in a few minutes. We'll get that out, and we'll head home."

Kenny nailed faster, swinging the hammer with

near lightning speed. He'd had enough of the wind pulling at his hat and whipping through his ears. He wasn't sure Texas ever got truly cold, but with this wind and the threatening gray sky, a chill skated over his arms.

The trucks arrived and the men set to work filling the troughs. Grass still grew in this field too, but no one would be out to check the herd for three days, and Garth wasn't the kind of foreman who took chances. Kenny knew he'd come out in a hailstorm to check on the cattle if he was concerned about them.

He finished up his job and helped get the last of the hay out. With fresh water in the lower trough, Garth called, "Let's get outta here, boys!" He flattened his hand against his head as the wind kicked up, and Kenny started toward his horse. He led two along behind him as a couple of the boys got a ride in the back of the truck.

"You okay there, Kenny?" Garth asked as he leaned out the window of the truck.

"Just fine, boss."

"It's just you and Aaron. Keep an eye on each other."

"Sure thing, boss." But Kenny didn't look up. The weather threw dust and dirt and debris into his face, and he used his cowboy hat to keep himself protected. At one point, he spotted Aaron ahead of him on the horizon, also leading two horses. Kenny whistled a tune he'd learned in the Marines as Orion, his faithful black-and-white horse, plodded on home.

He'd just passed the cabin in section twelve when something floated to him on the wind. He jerked his head up, searching for the source of the cry. Maybe it was an animal—the prairie played home to more than just cattle, he knew.

His pulse pounding and his blood beating through his veins, he scanned the horizon. Nothing.

The cry came again, a high-pitched noise without shape or meaning. He whipped his head left, and there, so far out where the land met the angry sky, he spotted a dark figure.

A human figure.

Chapter Two

Taryn wasn't sure if the water on her face came from her eyes or from the sky. All she knew was that the thunderous gallop of three horses was bearing down on her. An impressive man rode one of the beasts, like a Greek god from the movies she'd loved in college.

"What are you doing out here?" he asked, and her brain registered his voice as familiar.

"Kenny?"

"Taryn?" He swung out of the saddle and hurried toward her. "Why are you out this far?"

"I may have decided to take a walk during lunch and got turned around." She glanced in a near three-sixty-degree circle. "Everything out here looks the same."

He swept an arm around her shoulders and drew

her into his wall of a body. The wind chill factor dropped. In fact, the temperature on the plains suddenly rose ten degrees. "You're an hour from the homestead. How long have you been out here?"

"A while," she admitted. She didn't necessarily want to wilt into his arms, but her body acted of its own accord. She gripped the front of his shirt and sampled a breath of his musky, masculine scent. "I'm glad you spotted me."

"I wouldn't have if you hadn't been yelling."

She gazed up at him and locked onto his stormy eyes. She nearly fell at that moment, but managed to keep herself upright with only a slight stumble. "I wasn't yelling."

Concern flashed in his eyes at the same time lightning split the sky. He looked to his right, then his left. "Come on." He secured her hand in one of his and kept his grip on the reins of three horses in the other. "We'll never make it back to the ranch before the rain hits." Even as he spoke, the first drops peppered Taryn's forearm.

"Where are we going?"

"There's a cabin about two hundred yards back this way."

Taryn peered into the murky sky but couldn't see much more than gray soup. "You sure?"

"Dead certain."

Kenny moved with the liquid grace of an athlete, of a man who knew how to keep his body in peak operating condition—and had done so for a while. Taryn had to practically run to keep up with his long strides, a fact she became grateful for when the rain really started falling in earnest.

"Here." He all but shoved her into the cabin before ducking back into the storm to secure the horses. She heard him around the back of the structure, and she hoped the horses at least had some sort of shed to protect them from the weather.

The cabin consisted of one room, with the capability to curtain it into two. A stove sat against the back wall, and Taryn wondered if there was any dry wood to be had. A long counter ran along the wall to her right, and she wandered that way, the single cot on the opposite side of the cabin too dangerous to approach.

Kenny burst into the cabin a few minutes later, water dripping from his cowboy hat. He slammed the door behind him and secured it with two sliding locks, as well as a chain. "Wow! It's comin' down hard out there." He shook his hat off in time to the rhythm of the rain pelting the roof.

Taryn rubbed her arms and pressed herself against the back wall where the counter met wood. "So we're going to just...stay here until the storm settles, right?"

The cabin had two windows in the front, and one

on each end, but nothing in the back. Kenny peered out one of the front panes. "Could be a long time." He checked his watch. "It's almost dark as it is."

He turned back to her, a half-smile on his face. "I think we'll probably be here all night."

Taryn's throat turned to dust. "All night?" she managed to choke out. She glanced around wildly, like the cabin would suddenly transform and provide her with a hot bath, a private bedroom, and silk pajamas. "How is that possible?"

Kenny chuckled as he stepped to a wardrobe in the opposite corner that Taryn hadn't seen. "We've got blankets here. Some emergency food. A radio. I'll call in and let Garth know where I am. We'll be fine until morning."

"I can't stay out here all night." She eyed the single cot like it had done her wrong.

Kenny tossed two blankets onto the cot and raised his eyes to hers. "Why not?"

Did he really not get it? There was one bed. Two of them. *Emergency* food—surely that tasted about as good as it sounded. No wood.

"Can we light that stove?" she asked.

"Demanding little thing, aren't you?" He added a genuine laugh to the end of his statement, and Taryn got caught up in the warmth of it. How could he be so cavalier about this? Was he always so good-natured?

"There's wood in the shed out back," he said. "I shoved the horses in there too." He rooted around in the closet. "But here's some pellets for them. I'll go feed 'em, and bring in the wood." He grinned at her. "You can make your bed." He produced a sleeping bag, and Taryn was beginning to think that wardrobe was a cousin of Mary Poppins's tote bag. "I'll sleep on the floor."

He zipped over to the front door, unchained it, and darted into the storm before Taryn could put two words together. The man's energy almost unnerved her. She'd cleaned two cabins today before getting lost, and the weight of her exhaustion had her crossing the room and flopping onto the unmade cot without another thought.

Kenny found her there, and he stopped by the wardrobe before approaching her. "You should eat something." He held out a silver package.

She took it, but the thought of putting whatever it held in her mouth made her stomach revolt.

"You're not goin' into shock, are you?" Kenny crouched in front of her and examined her face. "I totally think you are. You look pale." He reached up and brushed her hair from the side of her face. "You need to eat and drink. And get up. Come help me start this fire." He gently placed his hand in hers, and she let him lead her to the pot-bellied stove. In fact, she would've gone anywhere with him at that moment. Strong, and sure, and smelling so good, Kenny seemed like the knight in shining armor Taryn needed in her life.

She listened to the bass timbre of his voice as he instructed her to place the wood just so, to crumple up the newspaper they kept stored at the cabin, to strike the match. She moved in a methodical way to match his voice, and before she knew it, the heat of the flames licked her face. She grinned and tipped her head toward Kenny's.

With only inches between them, Taryn froze. The happiness in Kenny's eyes brought tears to hers. She'd been happy like that before too. But not now.

"Hey," he said, swiping his thumb under her eyes. "Don't cry, now. I'm no good with beautiful women who cry."

She employed every ounce of self-control she had and willed the tears back into her chest, where they thankfully stayed. "I'm so glad you found me," she said again. "I don't think I would've ever found this cabin, and I certainly wouldn't have survived out here all night." A gust of wind shook the cabin, emphasizing her statement. She shivered with the thought of what would've happened to her had he not seen her.

"It's a miracle," he whispered. "Do you believe in miracles, Taryn?" The earnest way he watched her spoke to her soul, and now the flames in the room weren't only coming from the stove.

"Yes," Taryn said. "I believe in miracles."

Kenny's lips spread into a smile, and Taryn wondered what they'd feel like against hers. Startled at the thought of kissing a near-stranger, she cleared her throat and turned away. "Okay, let's get this place set up for tonight." Already the light was almost gone, and Kenny rummaged through the closet until he found a flashlight with the weakest beam Taryn had ever seen.

Still, it was enough to get the blankets on the cot, and the cot in front of the fire. Kenny gave her two bottles of water and told her to drink them before she fell asleep. He spread his sleeping bag just behind her cot, and if she let her arm slip over the side, she could hold his hand. Thoughts of doing so entertained her while she ate the protein bar he'd given her and drank her water. She watched the flames in the stove play together while she considered what to do with the feelings of attraction sparking between her and this marine cowboy.

No matter what she came up with, she knew she'd end up getting burned.

KENNY COULDN'T STAND the silence in the cabin. Well, it wasn't completely quiet. The rain created a symphony with the fire spitting in the stove.

"How long you been in Three Rivers?" he asked, his curiosity on the matter unending.

"About a week." The sadness in her voice, the fear he'd seen in her eyes, the way she cried so easily, told Kenny to tread lightly and be careful with her. At the same time, he wanted to see if he could make it to a fourth date with Taryn, a feat he hadn't accomplished in a while with any woman.

"What brought you here?"

"I needed a job." She sighed, the sound adding music to the cacophony of nature sounds. "Well, and the town's Halloween festivities lured me in."

"Oh, you like Halloween?"

"Not particularly." She turned toward him, and the fire backlit her face. "But the joy permeating this town.... The way everyone seemed to know everyone else, and the whole community came together." She barely lifted her top shoulder. "I liked how it felt here. So I decided to stay."

Kenny basked in the warmth of her story. "Three Rivers is a magical place," he agreed. "Where'd you come from?"

"Here and there."

He couldn't see her face, but the closed-off tone of

her voice probably would've manifested in an icy glare in those luxurious brown eyes. He much preferred them to swim with heat, soften like melted chocolate, the way they had just before a tear had escaped.

"I'm from California originally," he said, deciding to fill the silence with his own story. Seemed like Taryn didn't want to talk much, though he did wonder what kind of woman could roam the panhandle of Texas until she found a town she felt like staying in. "Served in the Marines for almost ten years. I got out of active service about three years ago, and my dad knew the foreman down here. Ranching seemed as good as anything else I might do with my life." He spoke to the ceiling as an overwhelming feeling of peace flowed through him. He hadn't known what to do when he'd graduated high school, thus the enlisting in the Marines.

And almost nine years later when he got released, he still hadn't known. But he knew now—God had led him to Three Rivers. He loved the small town. Loved that some of the roads in the older part of town were only wide enough for one car. Loved the quaint atmosphere of country living. Loved that he could feel things here that he couldn't in the city, because it was quieter and slower and simpler.

"You sound like you love it here," she said.

"I do." He chanced a glance at her, but she'd rolled

onto her back too. "You will too, Taryn," he promised. "Like I said, there's something healing and magical about Three Rivers."

Several heartbeats passed, broken when she said, "That's exactly what I need."

Kenny could feel it. Her tension rode in her shoulders, in the tense lines around her kissable mouth, in the way she so easily wandered away from a ranch and couldn't get back.

He woke sometime later, unable to distinguish between having his eyes open or closed. "Taryn?" he whispered.

"The fire went out," she hissed back. "It's freezing in here."

The chill of Kenny's nose suddenly felt like it had been frozen in liquid nitrogen. "I'll get it going again." He got up and felt his way past the cot only to find her kneeling in front of the dark stove too.

"I can't see anything." Something thunked to the ground. "And the flashlight went out five minutes ago." Panic edged her words, and Kenny fumbled his hands through the air until they met her body.

He recognized the shape of her shoulders, her arms, and threaded his fingers through hers. "Hey, it's okay."

She sniffed, and Kenny wanted nothing more than to protect her from everything ugly in her world, both past, present, and future. "I'll take care of it," he said, supremely glad "you" hadn't slipped into the sentence instead of "it."

He felt around on the ground where they'd left the newspaper and matches. His fingers found the right shapes and he struck a match and lit a piece of paper. The flame burned hot and bright—and fast—illuminating the items he needed. He memorized their locations and tossed the burning paper into the stove.

With the precision of a marine, he put in two pieces of wood, stuffed in balls of newspaper, and struck another match. Within a few minutes, a fire blazed in the stove. "There." He sat back on his haunches, pleased with his work.

Taryn sat cross-legged on the floor next to him. "Nice work, Marine."

"Do I detect a hint of sarcasm?" He hoped it wasn't disdain.

"Not at all."

"You wanted a fire. I gave you a fire."

"I want a lot of things." She hugged her knees to her chest.

Feeling brave, the way he had while in active service, he reached for her hand and cradled it in his. "What do you want, Taryn?"

She lifted that shoulder again in a shrug Kenny found sexier every time she did it.

"How about goin' out with me?" he asked, encouraged at the fact that she hadn't pulled her hand away. In fact, she'd matched her fingers to his. "Is that something you might want?"

She turned toward him, and it seemed to take a long time for her eyes to meet his. He didn't look away, though the intense feelings cascading through him evoked more fear than he'd ever felt before—even in Qatar.

"Yeah, sure," she said. "Why not?"

It wasn't exactly the answer Kenny had hoped for, but it would do. He grinned as he focused back on the fire, as Taryn did too, as she leaned her head against his bicep and breathed with him.

Chapter Three

"Kenny, come back." The tinny, male voice roused Taryn from sleep.

"Kenny, here." His voice came from further away than the sleeping bag he'd used the night before.

"The rain's lightened enough to get back. You should leave right now. Over."

"I'll saddle the horses and be there in an hour. Over."

"We've got the floodlights on. Over."

"Acknowledged. Over." His footsteps came closer. "Taryn?"

She could get used to waking up and having the first thing she saw be his gorgeous face, those cut arms. "I'm awake."

"We need to go. I have everything packed and ready except your blankets."

She scrambled to a seated position and smiled. "I'll take care of these while you get the horses ready." The thought of riding one almost sent her pulse into a frenzy, but she forced the anxiety back. She couldn't let every little thing push her over the edge of panic. Not anymore.

"They go in that closet. You can leave the cot there." He moved toward the door. "I put water on the fire a half hour ago. We're good to go." He unchained the door and peered into the atmosphere. "It's still raining, but it's more like a drizzle."

"I'll meet you outside."

"Sounds good." He ducked through the doorway and disappeared. Taryn did as she said she would and met him out front, where sure enough, he boosted her into the saddle of a horse. The ride back was miserable, with wind and rain driving into her face from time to time. Conversation couldn't happen, but that suited Taryn just fine. She felt like she'd already revealed too much to Kenny, too soon. But he hadn't seemed turned off. Just the opposite, in fact.

She allowed her thoughts to wander, and strangely they didn't automatically go to the negative events of her recent past. Instead, she contemplated the feelings she'd had while trying to sleep last night. Feelings of contentment of living here—permanently. Feelings of attraction for the handsome marine who'd asked her out. Feelings of uncertainty that she could have this town and this man in her life when so much of it existed up in the air.

Pushing the worries away, she made it back to the ranch, back to her apartment, and into her warm shower.

Her phone rang as she finished toweling her hair, and her blood turned to ice. She eyed the phone like it would be her old boss—or worse, Chris—calling. She didn't recognize the number, and she chose not to answer.

The call went to voicemail—which Taryn had also trained herself to delete without listening to—and the phone immediately began ringing again.

A peaceful feeling reminded her that she'd given her number to Kenny before leaving the ranch. She swiped on the call, the hope it would be him soaring toward the ceiling. When had she last let a man turn her into putty so fast?

"Hello?" she said much more hesitantly than she would've liked. She straightened her shoulders and looked into her own eyes. *Be strong*, she told herself as Kenny said, "Hey, there. Just checkin' to see if you made it home okay. The rain really started up again as soon as you left the ranch."

She leaned against the counter in the bathroom, the smile spreading across her face spontaneous and uncontrollable. "Had to use the wipers on double-time, but I made it."

"That's great." He wore a smile in his words. "So we never planned a time to get together."

"Oh, I'll be out at the ranch tomorrow," she said.

"You will?"

"Yeah, I work there, remember?"

"You can't come tomorrow."

"Why not?"

"The weather, remember?" He chuckled. "Surely you're not going to drive in that."

"It's a little rain," she said. "I have a job to do." And she'd already lost today's hours. She couldn't afford to miss another day. "We can maybe eat lunch together. Do cowhands eat lunch?"

"Usually in a big group, at one of the homesteads. My guess is Miss Kelly will have lunch for us tomorrow."

Taryn's stomach swooped at the mention of a big group. Last year at this time, she would've been on Chris's arm. And he was fun, and flirty, and the life of any gathering. She'd always been more reserved naturally, bringing out the act of perfection whenever the cameras switched on. But she loved being on the arm of the most popular man at the party.

"Oh, well, another day then."

"What? No," he said. "I'd gladly skip if you wanted

to sneak off to the barn or something. We can eat in the hayloft, stay out of the rain."

"Ooh, a hayloft. Sounds risky."

Kenny laughed, the booming sound warming her across the distance between them. "The ladder is a bit rickety. I'll fix it in the morning."

She giggled. "You don't need to fix the ladder for me."

"I'd fix anything for you," he said, his voice serious and quiet. So quiet, Taryn wondered if she'd heard him right.

Her reporter mind thought quickly and she said, "Well, I might just take you up on that, Sergeant Stockton."

A pause on the other end of the line made her think perhaps he didn't appreciate her brand of flirting. Then he said, "How'd you know I was a sergeant?"

"You left the closet door open," she blurted, totally not employing her quick thinking reporter brain. Even something like *Lucky guess* would've been better than saying she'd snooped through the man's closet mere minutes after walking in on him as he got dressed.

"I just saw the uniform. My brother—" She clamped her lips shut two words too late.

"It's okay," he said quickly to fill the gap. "Tell me later. And I did leave my closet open. Thanks for closing that. And, you know, for making my bathroom sink white again." He chuckled nervously and cleared his throat. "I actually have another favor that might send you running for the hills."

"Oh, I don't run," Taryn said, beyond relieved for his kindness in covering up her flub. The man was obviously made of patience—and a little dirt. She smiled at the memory of scrubbing his bathroom. "Unless there are large dogs chasing me. Will there be large dogs involved in this favor?"

His laughter came quickly, and she loved the joy emanating from him. She marveled at how easily he radiated such happiness, even over a phone line. "No dogs," he promised. "Well, maybe a couple of dogs. But they're old, and barely move, and I think even you could outrun them."

"So what's the favor?"

"Since my family is so far away, I usually stay here for the holidays. I go to my friend's house for Thanksgiving dinner, and his mom just asked how many would be coming." He paused, and Taryn's reporter radar went off.

"And?"

"And Charlie has a girlfriend this year, and I don't want to be the third wheel. That, or get seated at the kid's table because I'm a singleton. Believe me, it's happened. And I have a hard time fitting my legs under those tiny tables."

Taryn couldn't help the laugh that burst from her mouth. "I'll bet." She tried to imagine the towering, wide marine squishing himself in with ten-year-olds.

"Wondered if you had anywhere to go for Thanksgiving."

"As a matter of fact, I...don't." Of course, Taryn didn't even know if she'd still be in town in three weeks, when Thanksgiving rolled around. With a fierceness of thought she hadn't possessed since going for the nightly anchor position in Corpus Christi, she determined that she *would* be in Three Rivers for Thanksgiving.

"Great," Kenny said. "So we can go together. His family's in Amarillo."

Taryn swallowed. "Amarillo. Fantastic." But it so wasn't fantastic. She'd avoided cities with more than fifty thousand people, where the newscaster world narrowed and everyone knew everyone else. She tugged at the ends of her dyed-black hair. It was one meal. Behind closed doors. She looked completely different now than she did six months ago.

"You been to Amarillo?" he asked.

"No."

"Perfect," he said, but she wasn't sure why he thought so. "Okay, I have to go. See you tomorrow. Unless it's raining too hard. Then you should stay home."

He hung on the line, and she said, "I'll see you tomorrow, Kenny. Good-night." She pressed her eyes closed and hugged her phone to her heartbeat. If she let this gentle giant of a man into her life, what pain would she have to endure when they broke up? How far would she have to run?

Maybe you won't break up, she thought as she snuggled into the couch with a blanket and the television set on low volume. Her first impulse was to scoff at the thought. She'd broken up with every man who'd even gotten close to talking about a long-term commitment. Some very publicly.

Her second thought was, *Have faith.* She seized onto that one, because it felt more hopeful, more helpful, than her usual self-depreciation.

* * *

WITH ONLY TWENTY minutes of his lunch break left, Kenny paced in the barn. He hadn't seen Taryn around the ranch that day, his calls went unanswered, and he wasn't entirely sure what her car looked like.

"You're trying too hard," he muttered to himself. "You'll scare her off before you've even had a chance to get to know her." He gripped his phone, but he refused to call her again. Twice was enough. She knew where the barn was. She knew what time his lunch break started and ended.

He checked his phone again, just to be sure he hadn't missed her. That would be easier to swallow than her outright rejection. Hadn't missed her. His chest tightened and his stride lengthened.

The door opened, and he spun toward it, his heart galloping against this ribcage.

A woman moved toward him, and it only took Kenny a few steps for him to recognize Taryn. "You came," he said as she stalled several feet from him.

"I wasn't going to." She scuffed her feet against the floor; the sound reverberated against Kenny's pulse.

"Why did you then?" His words came out with too much bite, but he couldn't help it.

She moved a couple of steps closer. Close enough to see the worried look in her eyes and the tension in her neck. "You're so cute," she said. "I was nervous. Took a while to get over my anxiety and get myself over here."

He simply stared at her. *She* was nervous about spending time with him?

She glanced up to the loft. "So, have you eaten?" Her eyes came back to his, hooking and drawing him closer, deeper, farther than he knew a gaze could transport someone.

He lifted his brown paper sack, the top of which

had paid the price of his frustration. "Not yet." His throat felt dry and rough as sandpaper as he gestured her to go first up the ladder. It didn't emit a single creak, and a crack of satisfaction at his handiwork stole through him.

He followed her up, the scent of her perfume barely lingering in the air behind her. When he made it to the loft, she'd already settled her back against the wall, the round window immediately beside her.

Kenny took the spot on the other side of her and flashed her a winning smile. "I can't believe you think I'm cute." He pulled out his turkey sandwich and took a bite.

"Stop it." She smiled and opened a container of yogurt. She flipped the corner and mixed in the toppings.

He swallowed and nudged her shoulder with his. "Here I was thinkin' about how I could tell you how beautiful I think you are."

She blinked at him, her long lashes catching the light and throwing it into his face. "You are, you know. Beautiful." Kenny's fingers tightened and he worked to release them before he squished his sandwich. "I want to know everything about you. Let's start with your family. Yeah?" He examined her face for signs of distress, a warning voice in his head telling him to go slow with Taryn Tucker.

She flinched slightly, and Kenny suddenly remembered the slip about her brother. "Never mind," he said. "Job? I mean, obviously, you're cleanin' out here right now, but...." He shut his mouth, and fast.

This conversation was a complete disaster. Had he really brought up her family again? And was he really going to say she must've had a better job before becoming a maid for two dozen cowhands? He shoved half his sandwich in his mouth, the remaining fifteen minutes of his lunch suddenly too long.

A light laugh started from beside him, causing horror to snake through his gut. "Sorry," he mumbled around bread and meat.

"It's fine, Kenny. My family is...a bit of a sore subject, but I can tell you the basics. Born and raised in South Dakota. My parents are still there." She scraped her plastic spoon around the edge of the yogurt container to get every last bit. "My brother, well, he passed away a few years ago. It's still hard for me to talk about. I was very close to him."

Kenny's hand acted of its own accord, moving up and around Taryn's shoulders, drawing her into the protective shield of his chest. Right where he wanted her to be. Right where he needed her to be.

"I'm sorry," he murmured. "What happened?"

She cleared her throat and remained stiff in his

arms. "He was an ex-Marine, like you. Became a police officer and was shot during a drug bust in Philly."

Pieces began to click around in Kenny's head. No wonder she'd snooped through his closet when she'd seen the hint of his desert cammies. He couldn't think of anything to say, just like he hadn't been able to when he'd attended Marcus's funeral, one of his fallen comrades-in-arms. All he'd been able to tell Marcus's mother was, "I'm sorry," and he repeated the sentiment to Taryn again.

She sagged against him, and he relished the feel of holding her close, inhaling her floral and sunshine scent, and having her company.

"Tell me about your family," she said.

"My parents are divorced," he said. "My dad moved back to his homestate of Montana, where he now lives. He met Garth there. My mom lives in California. She has a boyfriend, but I don't ask her much about him." Kenny's words began to hollow and he forced a measure of happiness back into them. "I have one older sister who's married and lives in California too. One younger brother who works for a software company in Japan."

"Japan? Wow."

Kenny chuckled. "I know, right? He keeps telling me to come visit, but...."

"But what?"

"I don't really like to travel."

She leaned away and cocked her head up at him. "Really? I love traveling."

"Oh, yeah? You've done a lot of it?"

"Yeah, sure, when I was a reporter—" Her eyes rounded and her voice cut into silence. An alarm went off on her wrist, and she frantically pressed the button on the side of her fitness tracker. "I have to get back to work."

"Okay." Kenny watched her scramble away from him and practically tumble down the ladder, wondering what demons haunted her and how he could vanquish them.

Chapter Four

Taryn kicked herself while she cleaned the last cabin of the day, while she drove back to her apartment, while she showered. If Kenny had any skills with a computer, he'd know who she was—everything about her—with a simple Google search.

She wasn't sure how she could ever face him again. And yet, she found her feet taking her to the horse barn the next day when her alarm alerted her that Kenny's lunchtime had started. He wasn't there, but at least neither was anyone else.

A horse wandered closer, and Taryn reached up to pat it. She didn't have much experience with horses, but this eggshell-colored beast seemed about as dangerous as a cotton ball. It snuffled, and Taryn smiled at the gentleness of the animal.

"It's almost done raining," she said. "You look like you'd like a good, long ride."

"Don't promise her it's almost done raining." Kenny's voice widened Taryn's smile and she turned halfway toward him. "It is going into winter, you know. Rains a lot here in the winter."

"Define 'a lot'. Down in Corpus Christi, it didn't rain much."

He leaned against the fence next to her and stroked the horse's neck. "Is that where you're from?"

"I lived there for a long time," she said, her throat closing but not as far as it sometimes did. Progress. "I was a news reporter."

"Like on TV?"

"Yes."

The horse snuffled again, and Kenny laughed. "Okay, Peony. I'll get you some sugar." He moved away from Taryn, and the comfort and peace he seemed to exude went with him. He returned a minute later, several cubes in his hand. He handed them to Taryn. "Give 'er one at a time, and don't be surprised if a big black fellow joins you. Hank adores sugar."

Taryn held out one sugar cube, and a squirrel of delight ran through her when the horse sucked it up with her lips. Sure enough, a tall, black horse stuck his head into Peony's stall a moment later.

"I'm gonna go eat," Kenny said. "It's been a long morning." He moved to the ladder and scaled it in only a few steps. Taryn spent several more minutes with the two horses, also feeling their strength and power give her the confidence she needed to follow Kenny to the hayloft.

She found him in her spot next to the window, so she took his place from yesterday and pulled out her peanut butter sandwich. "Do you have allergies?" she asked.

"Just to penicillin. Makes me throw up."

She bit into her lunch. "Chunky or creamy?"

"Chunky, always." He grinned down at her. "You?"

"Both. Creamy in cookies. Chunky on sandwiches. Also, I found this gourmet peanut butter in Corpus Christi once. It was a blend of chocolate and peanut butter in a jar." Taryn relaxed as she remembered the international shop, which boasted chocolate from all over the world, and soft drinks from all walks of life. She'd found the chocolate peanut butter on a back shelf, along with a hazelnut cream she'd adored.

"Sounds dangerous," he said.

"It definitely was to my waistline," she agreed with a little giggle.

He matched his laughter to hers and slid his hand

into hers. He leaned his head back against the barn wall and closed his eyes, that infectious smile still playing with his lips. Taryn watched him, searching inside herself for how she felt here, with him, holding his hand.

She identified peaceful, content, happy. And she hadn't felt anything like those emotions in so long, she could barely recognize them.

She copied him, determined to memorize how right being here with him felt so she could hold onto it for later.

"Thanks for being patient with me," she said, unsure of where the words came from.

His only answer came in the form of extra pressure on her fingers.

* * *

Taryn met Kenny in the barn every day that she worked out at the ranch. She did her grocery shopping in person for the first time since leaving Corpus Christi. She even did a little window shopping down Main Street as Thanksgiving approached.

Something about Three Rivers had infected her. Something good. Something she didn't want to leave in her rear-view mirror. It was more than Kenny Stockton, though the handsome cowboy played the biggest part in her love affair with the small town.

She held hands with him, told him about her childhood, even ventured into territory she used to deem dangerous when she spoke briefly about Collin or her travels to various cities around the country.

The weeks passed quickly, until one day, Kenny said, "So I'll pick you up about eleven. Is that okay?"

"Tomorrow?"

"It's Thanksgiving Day tomorrow." He peered at her with curiosity. "Do you even own a calendar?"

She lifted her wrist and shook her fitness tracker at him. "I know what day it is."

"Do you?" He chuckled. "So eleven o'clock tomorrow. I'll need your address."

Taryn startled, unsure if she even knew her address. "Okay, I live above the barber shop."

"You do? Aren't you worried about Old Man Tillman?"

Taryn searched his face but found nothing sinister. "Why would I be?"

"You know, *Sweeny Todd?*" He smiled and tucked her closer to his body. "Never mind. Shouldn't have brought it up."

"Yeah, because now I'll be worried that that eighty-year-old man could climb the stairs." She laughed. "Which he can't, by the way."

Kenny laughed, the sound originating in his chest and vibrating Taryn's body. She loved listening to him laugh. She wished she could bottle the sound and fall asleep to it at night.

"Eleven is fine," she said. "What do I wear?"

"Whatever," he said. "Charlie's mom isn't fussy."

"So jeans would be okay?"

"Sure. That would be okay." He gestured to her disgusting maid clothes.

She leaned out of his arms. "This shirt has holes in the bottom of it."

He licked his lips—completely distracting her—and shrugged. "I like whatever you wear."

"You like whatever I wear?" She tipped her head back and laughed. "All you've seen is raggedy jeans and holey shirts."

"Not true. I saw you in that dress last week at church."

She wondered which one, because she'd left most of her nice clothes down south. "And you didn't come sit by me? I've been sitting alone for weeks. It's...."

"It's what?"

"It would be better if I had a handsome man to hold my hand during the sermon."

His gaze sharpened; he looked at her with all the precision of a predatory bird. A true marine. "Well, if I'd known that, I would've done it weeks ago."

His intense gaze combined with his husky words drove Taryn's desire toward the ceiling. Her eyes dropped to his mouth, her fantasies about kissing him taking center stage in her mind. Could she kiss him here? In a hayloft?

He dipped his head as if he'd meet her mouth with his right this second. She closed her eyes in anticipation, almost desperate for his kiss.

"So eleven tomorrow," he whispered, his mouth missing hers completely and touching just below her jaw. "And church on Sunday." His lips arced up toward her ear. "Yeah?"

"Yeah," she echoed, her voice hardly her own. He straightened, and she released the unconscious grip she had on his collar. He looked at her with desire and knowledge in his eyes, stood, and headed toward the ladder.

"'Bye, Taryn."

"See you tomorrow," she said, glad she knew Kenny wanted to kiss her as much as she wanted to kiss him. An equal measure of fear bolted through her. She knew what came after kissing, and that dating then led to proposals, and Taryn didn't have a great track record with those. Sighing, she followed Kenny's scent down the ladder to the horse stalls, where her newfound friends waited for her with eager eyes. At least they only wanted sugar cubes.

If Taryn could figure out what she wanted, she could at least take a step forward. As it was, she felt stuck. Stuck, with nowhere else to go. Nothing else to do.

* * *

KENNY MUTTERED to himself during the entire forty-minute drive to town. Charlie had left the ranch last night, so Kenny'd been alone in the cabin. His speeches then hadn't benefitted him any more than his stern self-lectures were helping him now.

He'd coached himself to go slow with Taryn, draw out the details of her life the way he would interrogate a prisoner, let her set the pace with their physical relationship. He'd wanted so badly to kiss her in the hayloft the day before. She wanted him to as well. Why he hadn't done it, he still wasn't sure.

Yes, he was. He hadn't kissed her because he had the feeling he shouldn't. He wasn't perfect at listening to the Lord and obeying, but he'd been trying really hard to do so when it came to Taryn. He prayed for clarity of thought when it came to her, and though his body had been screaming at him to *kiss her!* his mind had warned him to *back off*.

Kenny hadn't made it to kissing ground in a while —that usually happened after the third date with the women in Three Rivers. He could navigate the town's roads without thought, but he didn't know how to map this terrain with someone as complicated as Taryn.

In the end, he knew she needed to come to him. Whenever she was ready. He'd admit he'd prayed for quite a while last night that she would be ready soon. He didn't know how many more lunches he could endure without being able to taste her lips.

"At least one more, Marine," he ordered himself as he eased to a stop in front of the barber shop. He opened the door and stood just as a door to the right of the shop opened and a vision of poise and beauty emerged.

"Taryn," he breathed. No wonder the woman had been on TV. Wearing a denim dress with a wide, mustard-yellow sash, she looked sophisticated and kissable at the same time. He swept her into his arms, where she giggled and lifted her sandaled feet off the ground.

He nuzzled his face into her neck, taking a deep breath of her clean, crisp perfume. A new scent she didn't wear to clean cabins. "Mmm, Happy Thanksgiving, Taryn."

"Happy Thanksgiving, Kenny." She regained her feet and beamed up at him. "You look handsome as ever."

"That wasn't the dress I saw you wearing at

church." That one had been black, accentuated all her curves, and accented with bright blue jewelry.

"That's because I just bought it from the boutique." She indicated a building down the block. "The owner there is an amazing woman."

"*You're* an amazing woman." He took both her hands in his, beyond joyful to share this day with her.

She stretched up and brushed her lips across his cheek. "Thank you." Her southern twang pierced him right through the heart, and Kenny felt himself falling.

Not so fast, he told himself. Again, and again. He always fell first, and he didn't want to make that same mistake this time. He'd been treading so carefully, because he didn't want to make any mistakes with Taryn. She seemed like the type of woman who'd already seen her fair share of disappointments, and he didn't want to add to those.

"You ready to go?" he asked with a squeeze to her fingers.

"Not quite."

Kenny's eyebrows rose. "No?" He glanced back to the door through which she'd exited. "Did you need to run back upstairs?"

A playful glint rode in her eyes when he looked at her again. "Nope." She leaned forward, and he encircled her in his arms. She tipped onto her toes again, her eyes drifting closed a moment before Kenny under-stood her meaning.

Her mouth brushed his, incensing his desire for her. He brought her closer, catching her lips again and keeping them next to his for longer.

His pulse skyrocketed, but he forced himself to remain in the moment. Because it was the single best moment of his life.

Chapter Five

Kissing Kenny took the number one spot on Taryn's Best Experiences list. Previous to the uniting of their mouths, her trip to Iceland had claimed that spot. But now, standing with his muscular arms around her and his scent tantalizing her and his mouth so perfectly molded to hers, Taryn knew Iceland didn't hold a candle to Kenny Stockton.

Nothing ever would. No one ever could.

She finally broke the contact between them, her calves tense from having to stretch up to reach his face. He held her up easily, and she relaxed against his chest.

"Well...what was that?" he asked.

"Oh, I'm sorry. You didn't want me to kiss you?" She tipped her head back to look at him. "You sure acted like you liked it."

"Oh, I liked it." He ducked his head as if he'd kiss her again. But he didn't, and a knife of disappointment cut through her chest. "Just didn't know that had to be done before you could go to Thanksgiving dinner."

She stepped out of his arms, taking a careful moment to make sure her legs could support her weight. She smoothed down her skirt and adjusted her sash, which had been slightly displaced because of his grip on her waist. "Well, it did."

He stepped to her truck door and opened it. "So if I did that again, you wouldn't mind?"

Taryn moved into his personal space, her eyes caught on his. Desire and joy and a sparkling tease adorned his stormy-sky eyes. She lifted one shoulder in a nonchalant shrug. "I guess not."

She climbed into the truck as he said, "You guess not?"

"You'll have to try it and see." She crossed her legs and stared straight out the windshield. His chuckle made her grin as he closed the door and waltzed in front of the truck.

He got in next to her and started the ignition. He fiddled with the heater settings. He leaned across the space between them and tucked his hand behind her head. She turned toward him, letting him guide her mouth to his for the second best experience of her life.

An edge of fear started to wedge its way into her

mind, but she forced it away. She was just kissing a man. A man whose chest housed a heart of gold. A man who knew how to work hard, how to sacrifice, how to kiss a woman like he meant it.

He pulled away first this time, a smile already stuck to his face. "Yeah, okay, that had to be done before we go to lunch. But now we're late."

"Your fault," she said. "We had time for my kiss."

He laughed, the booming sound filling the cab. Against her will, she joined him, but her higher, more delicate laughter couldn't match his. She didn't even want it to. She reached over and tucked her hand in his, more content than she'd been in a long, long time.

He filled her in about Charlie and his girlfriend on the way to Amarillo, leaving Taryn to simply nod or agree in single-word sentences. Which she appreciated, but also didn't, because it let her mind wander down dangerous roads. Dangerous roads that reminded her that she wasn't ready for what came after kissing— and she didn't know if she ever would be.

* * *

THE NEXT TIME Kenny came to pick her up, Taryn let him come to the door and knock. "Come in!" she called as she searched her jewelry box for the pair of earrings she needed to make her outfit come together. She found the fish and put them on as Kenny's bootsteps stalled in her bedroom doorway.

"Hey, there."

The simple sound of his voice made her heart leap and her smile instantly appear. "Hey, yourself." She finished with her earrings and stepped into him for a kiss. He'd left her in her living room completely breathless on Thanksgiving evening. She hadn't seen him since, and though it had only been two days, she felt like perhaps a lifetime had passed.

Maybe she was ready for a new life. A new life in Three Rivers. A new life with Kenny. She pushed the thoughts to the back of her mind to deal with later. She'd met him a month ago; she certainly wouldn't be making any long-term decisions right away.

But maybe you should, she thought, which made her freeze.

"What?" Kenny asked.

"Nothing," she said quickly. Taryn certainly couldn't tell him that maybe they should put both feet on the accelerator and see what happened. She ducked her head, embarrassed at her own idea, though a remote corner of her mind kept screaming at her to do something different than she'd done before. And she'd never spent less than two years dating a man before, well, before breaking up with him.

She stole a glance at Kenny, who seemed wrapped

up in the artwork above her mantle. Taryn didn't want to break up with him. But she also knew that relationships with men as magnetic and charismatic as Kenny only ended in one other way—heartbreak.

He's worth it.

The thought didn't seem to belong to her, but she listened to it anyway. As she led him downstairs to his truck, she realized that her heart hadn't been broken when she ended things with Chris. No, her pride had been wounded. Her reputation called into question. But she hadn't been heartbroken.

The distinction became important as she entered the chapel with Kenny on her arm, as the pastor started his sermon, as she realized that she'd run away from her own humiliation. Not from Chris. Not from her job. But from herself.

TARYN SEEMED to be lost inside her own head. When the pastor cracked a slight joke during his sermon, she didn't even smile. Like she hadn't even heard him. As the minutes passed, Kenny realized his assessment was spot-on. She wasn't listening, but she seemed alert and tense, which meant she'd disappeared inside herself again.

Kenny let her drift, though he wished he could see

inside her head and straighten everything out. Instead, he focused on what the pastor had to say the Sabbath after Thanksgiving.

"As we move into the season where we celebrate the birth of the Savior, let us remember how He lived, and strive to emulate Him in our own lives."

Kenny found himself nodding along with most of the congregation. The pastor ended soon after, and he nudged Taryn toward the aisle. But she didn't budge, being surprisingly strong for such a small woman.

"Kenny," she said. "Can you come back to my place for a few minutes? I have something...." She swallowed so hard, it required every muscle in her neck to do it. "I have to show you something."

Her anxiety bled into the air surrounding them, and Kenny found himself tensing as if he might be struck. "Sure," he managed to say. "What's up?"

"Just...something I've been thinking about."

He couldn't force himself to make trite conversation on the way back to her apartment, and she certainly didn't contribute anything. Kenny flexed his fingers on the steering wheel and prayed for patience and strength and for the right reaction and words to say.

She unlocked her door and took a deep breath before entering. "Okay, so I just want you to know this is hard for me, but I was sitting there in church, and I had a feeling I needed to be brave and show you why I came to town."

Kenny's heart twisted, ached, at the sight of pure fear on Taryn's face. He wanted to erase it and build a protective wall around her life so it could never come back. He drew her into his chest and wrapped her in his arms. "Whatever you want, Taryn."

She breathed beside him, the rising and falling of her chest matching his. "Okay. I'm going to get it set up, but I can't watch it again."

Kenny's throat felt like someone had poured sand into his mouth, like he was back in Qatar and couldn't get away from the heat and granules and agony. He watched, mute, as she opened her laptop and clicked, typed, clicked again.

"So I left Corpus Christi several months ago," she said, gesturing for him to take her place at the dining room table where she had her computer queued up. "This is why."

He sat, but he didn't look at the computer. "Taryn, I don't really care why you left Corpus Christi."

She graced him with a faint smile that barely touched her lips. "This is the twelfth town I've come to." Another hard swallow. "But it's the first where I actually want to stay. And the only way to do that is to show someone why I've been bouncing around for months."

He glanced at the laptop. She'd opened a YouTube video and paused it. The screen sat black and waiting for him. His stomach squirmed like it used to before a mission, and he steeled himself for whatever he was about to see.

"I want you to stay in town too," he said.

"You're the reason I want to stay," she whispered. "And that scares me more than anything. More than showing you this video. But at least then you'll have a better idea of who I am."

Kenny almost protested, but Taryn turned and left the room, closing her bedroom door behind her. A few moments later, the low beat of loud music shook the floor. Kenny faced the laptop like it was his target, something dangerous and to be feared.

He squared his shoulders and clicked the play button. Taryn appeared on the screen, her makeup and hair flawless, her smile bright, her words delivered with the practice and skill of someone who'd been on live TV for years. She was every bit the sophisticated professional he'd seen exit her apartment on Thanksgiving Day.

She ended the newscast, but the camera didn't fade into a commercial. Her co-anchor, a man named Harry Herbert, grinned as if he'd won the lottery, and said, "We have one more thing tonight, Taryn."

She maintained her professional smile, but Kenny saw the blip of panic in her eyes. "We do?"

Another man appeared on-set behind her, a tall, blond-haired man with blue diamond eyes. "Taryn Tucker." She spun toward him, her practiced professionalism fading as the man got down on one knee.

"Chris," she breathed, both hands pressing over her pulse. "What are you doing?" She shook her head, tiny little movements left and right that told Kenny she didn't want him to propose. Anyone would've picked up on her cues.

But apparently not Chris. He proposed, and Taryn said no.

Right there on air.

Harry's smile dropped. Chris looked at the camera with pain etched in his face. Taryn fled the set, and Harry closed the segment. The video faded to black.

Kenny sat back in his chair, his mind whirling through the three-minute video again. It didn't take long for him to decide he didn't care. He stood, the chair scraping loudly against the floor. His knock was answered with the music cutting off and Taryn opening the door.

"I don't know who that woman was." Kenny hooked his thumb over his shoulder. "But she isn't you." He inched into her personal space, pleased when she didn't shuffle back. "I'm glad you showed me, because it does explain why you've been so hesitant with me." He paused when she flinched like he'd flicked cold water in her face.

He backed up a couple of steps, enough for her to get out of her bedroom if she wanted to. "Talk to me."

"I dated Chris for two years," she said.

Kenny schooled his features into a mask of stone. He'd had many opportunities to keep his true feelings behind a solid wall. "So?"

"I...I have a hard time committing to someone."

"It's not like we're going to get married anytime soon." He crossed his arms. "We just met a month ago."

"I like you," she said.

He quirked one side of his mouth. "I like you, too."

"I don't want to be hesitant with you."

"I don't want you to be that way either." He relaxed, stuffing his hands into his pockets instead. "But I'm okay with whatever you want. If you just want to hold hands and kiss me, that's fine."

She ducked her head. "What if I just want to be friends?"

"No." Kenny didn't mean for his voice to sound like a bark, but it did. He moved toward her and embraced her. "No, I don't want to be just friends. I want to be your best friend, sure. The person who knows the most about you. Who can run to the store and get your favorite juice and that doughnut you like the most. But not *just* friends." He touched his mouth to the spot just below her jaw. "I like kissing you too much for that."

She tilted her head and kissed him. He felt something new in her kiss, something deeper, something more permanent. And he knew she didn't want to be just friends either.

In fact, that was probably why she'd shown him the video. Kenny catalogued the information, the feelings, and then lost himself in Taryn's kiss—something he wanted to do everyday of his life.

Chapter Six

Taryn enjoyed her work more than she thought possible. It felt nice, easy, relaxing, to just show up, do her job, and go home. She didn't have to be "on" all the time. She didn't have to look perfect, act perfect, sound perfect. It was freeing to just be Taryn, not Taryn-Tucker-of-Channel-Nine-News.

Kenny had taken the video in stride, and she wondered now why she thought he wouldn't. Everything he did he took in stride. The man was unflappable. It was as maddening as it was admirable.

"Hey there, gorgeous." He leaned in the doorway to the barn, delicious-looking in his cowboy boots, dark jeans, leather jacket, and his trademark cowboy hat.

She smiled but went back to stroking Peony. She'd felt something with the horses, a connection she'd never imagined could exist between a horse and a human. She'd done a little research into the thera-peutic riding facility housed at the ranch, and she had an appointment with Pete Marshall, the owner, that afternoon after she finished cleaning cabin three.

"I brought you something." Kenny sidled up to her and held out a pastry bag.

"Kenny." She stretched up and kissed him quick before taking the bag. "What is it?"

"You never did tell me what your favorite doughnut is. So I figured I'd buy one everyday until I landed on the right one."

"You drove to town this morning?" She glanced inside the bag and pulled out an apple fritter. "For this?"

"Ah, so it's not an apple fritter." He swiped the pastry from her fingers and took a big bite. "Good, because I love these things."

She laughed and reached for the fritter. "They're not my favorite, but I don't hate them." She took a bite too, a moan stretching from her throat. "Oh, this is fantastic."

"And I didn't drive to town," he said. "Miss Heidi is startin' a bakery, and her pastry chef has been bringing samples to the ranch for weeks."

"This is literally the best apple fritter I've ever eaten."

"I'll tell Grace. She'll be happy." Kenny smiled at

Taryn, the gesture more than just movement. It carried adoration and desire, joy and genuine warmth.

"How are you so happy all the time?" She nudged his shoulder with hers and lifted one foot to the bottom rung of the fence.

"Is that a bad thing?" Kenny clasped his hands and let them hang over the railing into the horse stall. His voice sounded measured and even, and Taryn suspected she'd hit a nerve.

"Have other people said it's a bad thing?"

"About every woman I've dated," he said. "The last one said she didn't want to go out with me again, because it was too hard to see me so happy when she wasn't. Said she actually felt guilty when she got home."

Taryn blinked at him, at the stoic expression on his face, at the way he stared down Peony like she was an enemy. Laughter pooled in her stomach and bubbled up through her throat.

"So that's funny to you, huh?" He kicked a smile in her direction.

"A little, yeah. You must not have kissed that other woman."

"Never made it that far, no."

Taryn linked her arm through his and pressed in close. "Good. Because if you had, she wouldn't care how happy you were. She'd just be thinking about the next time she could kiss you."

"So you're saying you can put up with my joviality because I'm a good kisser?" He peered down at her, that cowboy hat casting them both in shadows.

"You are a *great* kisser." She maneuvered into his arms, relieved when he held her tight and close, the way he always did. "And I like your joviality. It makes me think that I can be that happy one day too."

He kissed her forehead, his cowboy hat getting dislodged. He swiped it off to reveal his sandy hair. She traced her fingers along his ears and behind his neck. He touched his lips to the tip of her nose. "Why aren't you?"

Such a simple question, with such a complicated answer. As she thought about it, Taryn realized that happiness was a choice. That she didn't have to let the things from her past haunt her forever.

"I'm trying to be," she finally said. "I'm going to see Pete this afternoon. Maybe I'll be a cowboy like you."

"I like you just how you are." He beamed down at her and then kissed her. As she relaxed into his touch and deepened the kiss, Taryn recognized a definite vein of happiness threading through her.

She knew what she wanted. For the first time in a long time, she knew she wanted to live in Three Rivers. She wanted to spend as much time as possible with

Kenny Stockton. She wanted to be happy with Kenny, in Three Rivers.

Is that possible? she asked as Kenny led her up to the hayloft so they could eat lunch.

A distinct lesson from her childhood struck her full in the chest. *With God, anything is possible.*

KENNY ENJOYED his hour-long lunch more over the next couple of weeks than he ever had. Peanut butter and raspberry jam had never tasted so sweet, especially when it was what Taryn packed and he just got to taste it on her lips.

He spent his afternoons whistling and reliving the passionate kisses he shared with Taryn in the privacy of the hayloft. With two weeks until Christmas, he began to stew about what he should get her.

They were exclusive, that was certain. He was falling fast for her. Also certain. She seemed to enjoy his company as well, and she melted like butter over an open flame every time he touched her. He felt certain the feelings between them were mutual.

He'd actually started dreaming in diamonds, but he wouldn't be asking Taryn to marry him for Christmas. The very idea would drive her to another town in the dead of night. He also knew that for certain.

He could be patient. At least he told himself he could. Seeing her and kissing her five days a week helped. Six if he could get into town on Saturdays. But he never saw her on Fridays, so he put his head down, ate lunch alone in his cabin to avoid the ribbing by the other boys, and passed the hours until he could call Taryn and be soothed by her pretty little voice.

Near quittin' time on Friday, Kenny suddenly thought of the perfect gift for Taryn. His pace increased to get the animals fed for the evening so he could head into town and meet with his friend and travel agent, Jeremy Thacker.

Taryn loved to travel. Had done a bunch for her job, but he wanted this trip to be pure pleasure for her. They'd talked about her family, and his, and where she'd like to visit, and where he would, and Kenny practically burst with happiness at his plan.

Kitty Hawk, he recited as he threw hay and slopped water into troughs. He headed over to the administration trailer to check out with either Garth or Lawrence, the controller.

When he opened the door, he practically ran into the back of an older gentleman. The man stood in front of Lawrence's empty desk, holding his phone in one hand like he expected it to go off at any moment.

"Hey," Kenny said. "Has someone helped you?" This man had clearly never stepped foot on a ranch.

He wouldn't be wearing leather shoes shinier than the sun if he had.

"I'm looking for someone," he said, his deep voice commanding respect with only a few words.

"Is Lawrence helpin' you find them, or...?"

The man slid his appraising gaze from Kenny's cowboy hat to his cowboy boots. "Not yet."

"Maybe I can help you. Who you lookin' for?"

The man sighed like Kenny wasn't worthy of his attention. "I was told there's a woman here who cleans the cabins. Taryn Tucker?"

Alarms blared in Kenny's head. This man hadn't been on the video. He wasn't the co-anchor or the ex-boyfriend. So who was he?

"She doesn't work on Fridays," Kenny managed to say.

"Do you know where I can find her?"

Kenny didn't want to lie, but he reasoned that he didn't know for certain that Taryn would be at home. When he called her on Friday nights, she answered, and she usually said she'd spent the day cleaning or shopping or wandering the town. She could be *any*where.

"Sorry, I don't."

Kenny held his breath, hoping this guy wouldn't ask for her phone number. But someone else in the world must've needed a bigger miracle than his, because the man did ask.

Kenny leaned all his weight on his right leg, trying to figure out who this man was. In the end, he asked, "Who are you? I'm not sure she wants you to have her number if she didn't give it to you."

The man's eagle eyes sharpened, and he glared up at Kenny. "Taryn used to work for me. I'm not going to hurt her."

"In Corpus Christi?"

The man picked invisible lint from his impeccable suit. "You seem to know quite a bit about Taryn."

Kenny put on his mask. "She's worked here for a couple of months. We've eaten lunch together a few times, that's all."

"I'm not going to hurt her," he repeated.

"What do you want with her?"

"I need her back," he said.

A balloon of sub-zero liquid expanded in Kenny's chest. Taryn couldn't leave Three Rivers. He didn't want to be without her.

"She'll be in on Monday," Kenny said, perching on the edge of Lawrence's desk.

The man glared, and Kenny gave his attitude right back to him. It was obvious that this man was used to getting what he wanted, when he wanted it. But Kenny didn't care. He didn't have the right to give Taryn's phone number out to men whose names he didn't even know.

"Very well." The man turned on his designer heel and left the administration trailer. Kenny didn't waste another moment—he hurried down the aisle, his fingers already pulling up Taryn's number on his phone. He could get her a vacation tomorrow, but he wanted her to know about her old boss now. He wasn't sure what the fallout would be—*Please let her stay in town*, he prayed—but it was a risk he needed to take.

Her line rang while he continued a steady stream of silent prayers to keep her in his life. He would propose on Christmas Day if he thought Taryn was ready. But he knew she wasn't. Even with several sessions with Peony, she wasn't ready. And Kenny didn't want to end up like the boyfriend on the video he'd watched.

Pushing his own fears and insecurities aside, he muttered, "Come on, Taryn. Answer."

"Hey, there," she finally said, obvious happiness in her voice.

"Hey," he said. "So there was just a man here...."

Chapter Seven

Taryn had been in the triangle yoga pose when her phone started ringing. She'd almost let the call go to voicemail so she could keep the positive energy she'd been gathering. But in the end, something whispered to her to get up and get the phone.

Now, as she listened to Kenny talk, she wished she hadn't. Well, that wasn't quite true. She was really glad he'd called, she just didn't like what he had to say.

"Thanks, Kenny," she said when he finally finished. She'd never heard him speak so fast, with such urgency.

"What are you going to do?"

"I don't know."

"Do you want me to come in?"

"No," she said. "I'll deal with Stanley."

"Taryn," he started, and a twinge of annoyance twisted through her.

"It's fine, Kenny. I'm fine."

"I don't think you are."

Her annoyance bloomed into full-fledged frustration. He'd been kind to her; patient and gentle; never pushed her farther than she wanted to go. He let her initiate the hard conversations, and he kissed her whenever she felt like her world was about to implode. She'd come to rely on him, something she'd never really done with Chris—or anyone else in her life.

"This has nothing to do with you," she said.

"How can you say that?" Kenny exhaled, maybe the first angry sound she'd heard him make. "I'm in love with you. What happens to you affects me."

"I—" She stalled completely. He couldn't love her after only a few weeks together. Could he? She didn't even love herself yet, though her training with the horses had helped her in more ways than she could enumerate.

"Just tell me you're not going to leave town. That I'll pick you up for church on Sunday, and we'll go together, and then I'll be able to come back to your place and fall asleep on your couch while you make those meatballs I can't get enough of." His voice held a hint of desperation, a ton of anxiety, and his usual level of playfulness.

She found a smile pulling at her lips. "Of course I'll be here on Sunday," she said. "I'm not going anywhere, Kenny."

"Maybe I can come into town tomorrow."

"Don't worry so much," she said. "You'll ruin your perfectly handsome face." She took a deep breath. "I'll call Stanley, and I'll call you back."

"Okay," he said and they hung up. But Taryn didn't call Stanley immediately. She paced from her living room to her kitchen and back, biting her lip while her mind ran down a road she hadn't unleashed it on in months.

She knew why Stanley had tracked her down—he wanted her to come back. Kenny had confirmed Taryn's suspicion. She also knew Stanley was one of the most persuasive men on the planet. What he wanted he usually got. She was actually surprised that he hadn't been able to get her phone number from Kenny.

Her gaze fell on the sheaf of paperwork she needed to sign. The paperwork for her new house in Pinion Ridge, a new community going in on the southwest side of town. She hadn't told Kenny about it. Had wanted to surprise him on Christmas Day. She'd imagined the look on his face a hundred times.

"You need a plan," she told herself as she gripped her cell phone. "Stanley just won't accept a no."

But though she paced for another ten minutes, she couldn't come up with a plausible plan, an extraordinary excuse, nothing. She only knew she wanted to stay in Three Rivers. She'd fallen in love with the town, and she suspected she could fall in love with Kenny if she'd let herself.

Needing a bit more time, she texted Stanley that she'd meet him for dinner at the steakhouse—he'd be paying—and she stepped into the shower to put on her professional face.

SHE SAT IN THE BOOTH, her right leg bouncing a mile a minute. She'd waved the waitress away from refilling her water twice now, and she checked her phone again with a scowl. Stanley was almost thirty minutes late.

So typical. She glared out the window, but all she could see was her own displeased face. Five more minutes. And then she'd leave. She didn't owe him anything. She'd given her notice, worked out her last two weeks in the booth, and come back to town to get her final check. So she'd gone to the station in the middle of the night when she knew Stanley wouldn't be there. So what?

She didn't owe him anything.

Seven minutes later, she looped her purse over her

shoulder and stood. She turned toward the exit and came face-to-face with Stanley Summers. "You are so late," she growled. "I was just leaving." She brushed past him and held her head high as she strode toward the front doors.

"You know I'm a vegetarian," he said as he matched his stride to hers.

She burst into the night beyond the steakhouse, her breath seizing at the temperature difference. It never got this cold in Corpus Christi, though it still wasn't considered cold by most standards.

"I'm not coming back," she said.

"I need you. Our ratings have tanked since you left."

"I'm happy here."

He tugged on her arm, and she stopped to face him. "You're cleaning cowboy cabins."

"So what?"

"You have a degree in journalism. You're an excellent reporter."

"I'm really good at a lot of things." She folded her arms to protect herself from his penetrating gaze. "I'm not leaving town. I like it here."

Stanley glanced around like he couldn't fathom what she could possibly like about Three Rivers. "There's nothing for you here."

"I have a job here. Friends."

"Friends?" Stanley chuckled. "Taryn, you lived in Corpus Christi for two years before you knew your neighbor's first name."

"I'm not the same person anymore." She liked that Kenny thought she was someone different from the woman on the video. She wasn't that person anymore. She'd only existed in Corpus Christi, and Taryn didn't want to be her again.

"Name one friend you have here."

"Gene."

"Landlords don't count."

"Pete," she countered.

Stanley cocked his head in disbelief. "What about that Kenny cowboy?"

"Yeah, we're friends," she said, almost choking on the word.

"He's an awful lot like Chris." Stanley focused over her shoulder like anything and everything was more interesting than her.

"He is *nothing* like Chris." Taryn started toward her car again. "We're done here, Stanley. Go home." Just because Chris and Kenny both commanded attention didn't make them a lot alike.

"I can't go back without you." He stepped in front of her, effectively blocking the path to her car.

"I am not going with you." His insistence that she

return to Corpus Christi only fueled her fire to stay in Three Rivers.

"You've got to give me something. Your city needs a good-bye."

"I don't feel guilty about the way I left," she said. "I put in my two weeks."

"I needed you in front of the camera." He softened, showing his true age of almost seventy. "I still do."

She sighed and focused on the horizon to her right. "Three Rivers has quaint and festive celebrations during the holidays. Let's say, I...I don't know. Do a holiday spec piece for you. Then will you delete my number from your phone and never bother me again?"

A spark entered his eye. "You're telling me you— *the* Taryn Tucker—really wants to stay in this little town? How many people live here? Like five thousand?"

"I don't know," she said. "And I don't care. I like it here, and I'm tired of running." The thought of packing up her car again tied her lungs into knots.

"There's nothing to run from." He quieted his voice into that grandfatherly tone that had won her over many times. "Chris left town shortly after you. He hasn't come back, and no one misses him." He gave her a warm smile. "It's you they want to see."

She shook her head, the image of Kenny's chiseled face, the memory of his lips against hers too strong to give in. "I'll do the special. You can call it an op-ed piece. Whatever you want. But I'm doing it here, and that's it." She glared at him, though most of her ire had evaporated. "Now, please move so I can go home. I still need to eat since someone so rudely showed up terribly late."

Stanley's eyes burned with curiosity, with intelligence, with acceptance. He moved out of the way. "Send me a proposal for the piece. You can do whatever you want, but it has to include a proper good-bye to your people in Corpus Christi."

"Fine." She wrenched the car door open and dropped into the driver's seat. She roared out of the parking lot, her blood racing like it was trying to win a marathon. After a few blocks of erratic driving, she turned left when she should've gone right. The road out to the ranch had always soothed her, and tonight, as the street lights in town faded behind her, the stars in the wide, black sky twinkled like diamonds.

By the time she pulled up to Kenny's cabin, the peaceful countryside had worked its magic on her over-wrought system.

KENNY SULKED AROUND HIS CABIN, eating a frozen pizza by himself as Charlie was in town with his girlfriend again. He had the TV on loud, because while he usually enjoyed the serene quiet of the range, tonight the silence felt suffocating. His phone rested on his knee just to make sure he didn't miss a single buzz.

But none came.

He got up and made himself a cup of spiced apple cider and a stack of toast. He realized as he grumped around his kitchen that he was in a bad mood. He hadn't felt this way in such a long time, he barely recognized the anxiety twining through his stomach and the way everything from Charlie's dirty dishes to having to get out more butter made him frown.

His front door opened, and he turned toward the sound, surprised Charlie had returned so early.

But it wasn't Charlie standing in the doorway; it was Taryn.

"Do you even know how to knock?" he asked, his toast and cider completely forgotten. His foul mood seemed to have evaporated at the sight of her.

"I did." She stepped into the cabin and closed the door behind her. "Your TV is so loud, you obviously didn't hear me."

Kenny scanned her, searching for signs of distress. She said she'd call, not show up on his doorstep wearing her flawless makeup and high-quality clothes. Besides those differences, she seemed whole and healthy. Her dark eyes sparkled, and her hair had grown out over the past several weeks, revealing her naturally honey-blonde color.

"Did you talk to your boss?" he asked, maintaining his position in the kitchen.

"He's not my boss." She shrugged out of her coat and collapsed on his couch. After turning off the TV, she leaned back and closed her eyes. "He wants me to come back to the station."

Kenny practically ran to her side. "What—I mean, you're not—" He closed his mouth, wanting to tell her how much he needed her to stay in town until they could see this through, but not wanting to influence her too strongly. She needed to make her own decisions, choose her own path in life. He wanted to be part of that life, part of her decision-making process, but she needed to include him in that on her own.

"What are you going to do?" he asked.

Without opening her eyes, she snuggled into his side. "I like it here." She sounded sleepy and sexy, and Kenny's hand cupped her bicep and kept her close. "I'm not going back to newscasting, but I do need another job. I can't clean cowboy cabins forever."

He caressed her arm, his mind whirling. "Well, I'm not sure there's something for someone of your expertise in Three Rivers."

"Mm." She yawned. "I'll figure something out."

"So you're not leaving."

"No. Stanley really wants me to come back, and I agreed to do a special piece on the Christmas celebrations here in town in order to give my goodbyes to the people in Corpus Christi."

"And that's what you need to do?" He brushed his lips against her forehead. "Will that give you the closure you need?"

"I think so." She opened her eyes and glanced up at him. "So that's what I'm going to do. Stanley agreed to leave me alone after that."

He grinned, glad she'd come instead of called. Glad she was staying.

"Now, I believe we have something else to talk about." Her eyes burned with an emotion he couldn't quite name, and he'd gotten really good at reading her over the past couple of months.

"We do?"

"Yeah, you said something pretty heavy on the phone earlier."

His brow creased and he searched his memory for what he'd said. "Remind me."

She ducked her head and rested her cheek against his chest. "You said you were in love with me."

His heart catapulted to the back of his throat and back. "Well, I suppose I am."

"You *suppose* you are?"

"I shouldn't have said that," he said. "I know you're

not ready to hear it, and you certainly can't say it back. I guess…I guess it was just how I was feeling in that moment, because I was worried about you and wanted you to know you had someone in your corner."

He took a deep breath to force himself to be quiet, to allow himself some time to think, to give her a chance to consider what he'd said.

She breathed next to him, her shoulder rising and falling evenly. He enjoyed the silence with her, knowing for dead sure that he did love her. He shouldn't have said it, but that didn't mean he couldn't feel it.

"I have moments of loving you too," she said.

He flinched like she'd shouted. "You do?"

She heaved a sigh and sat up. "You're right—I'm not ready to say it back. I'm barely ready to hear it. But I want you to know that I feel strongly about you. And if you give me enough time, and keep kissing me when I'm unsure, I know there will come a day when we're on the same page at the same time."

"Did you just give me permission to kiss you whenever I want?" He quirked half a smile at her.

She giggled and pushed her palm against his chest. "You already do that."

"Oh, honey, trust me when I say I don't. If it were up to me, I'd kiss you a lot more." He leaned down, his mouth hovering dangerously over hers. Everything in her relaxed, sighed against him, submitted to his will. Her eyes drifted closed and her lips parted slightly, ready and waiting for him to kiss her.

He sat up straight, satisfied that he could keep kissing her—and nothing more—until she was ready to fully commit to him.

"Tease," she said, ducking her head again.

He lifted her chin and brought his mouth to hers firmly and kissed her with every ounce of passion and love he felt for her.

Chapter Eight

Taryn pulled into the parking lot in front of
Courage Reins on the last Friday before Christmas, ready for her therapy. Reese sat behind the desk,
looking tired and happy to see her at the same time.

"You okay?" she asked.

"No, but it's Friday."

"Is Carly in today?" Taryn glanced down the left
hall.

"No, she's gone to Amarillo for the weekend."
Reese's face lit up. "I'm heading out after work tonight.
A birth mom called her last night, and she left this
morning."

Taryn's heart lifted. "That's great news, Reese."
She knew the couple had been trying to adopt a baby
for a while now, but had had some disappointments
along the way. She felt connected to Reese and Carly

because of it. Same with Pete, who came down the right hall, which led to the indoor arena.

"Miss Taryn, I have Peony ready for you." He turned sideways and pointed down the hall. "You ready?"

She smiled at Reese and stepped past Pete. "Sure am." She pushed through the door. "When's that construction going to be done? What are they doing out there again?"

Pete helped her mount Peony. "It's a horse training facility, and the construction crew should be done tomorrow, I think. They've been pulling long hours to get it finished before the holidays." Pete handed her the reins. "Remember not to pull."

She appreciated that his entire lecture consisted of four words. She did like to pull on the reins, control the horse instead of working with it.

An idea had been percolating in her head since Stanley had come to town. She needed to film her piece tomorrow night, Christmas Eve. "Pete, isn't your mother-in-law opening a bakery soon?"

"Yeah. I've gained ten pounds since she's been experimenting with her recipes out here." He chuckled and patted his still-flat stomach. "Take 'er around a few times, and then we're going to gallop."

Taryn's heart dropped to her cowgirl boots, and she stayed still. "Can I get your mother-in-law's number? I want to talk to her about being in my editorial piece on small town Christmas celebrations." And she wanted to find out if she needed help in the bakery. Taryn liked coming out to the ranch and spending time with Kenny, but she really needed something else to keep her bills paid.

"Sure, I'll get it for you while you ride." He gave her a look that said, *Get going,* and Taryn clucked the horse into movement. She loved moving with the horse, talking to her like she could answer and give advice.

Feeling soothed and relaxed, Taryn slid to the ground at the end of her session. Kenny waited for her in the horse barn, where she brushed down Peony and fed her a sack of oats. "You want to go to dinner tonight?" he asked.

"I...can't." She didn't look at him. "I have tons of prep work to do for the piece tomorrow."

She hated the little fib. She did have loads to accomplish before tomorrow evening, when the camera crew would expect her to be ready to be on live TV— something she hadn't done in over eight months. But she could afford a few hours for dinner with her boyfriend.

Problem was, she already had an appointment with another man—the one giving her the keys to her new house out at Pinion Ridge.

"Can we get together tomorrow night, late, after I

film?" She'd be exhausted and stretched thin by then, and being around the perpetually joyful Kenny would be just what she needed.

"Yeah, sure. I'll be at the celebration, so we can just go from there."

She seized. "You'll be at the celebration?"

He chuckled and pulled her into his chest. "Taryn, everyone in town knows about the camera crew coming for the feature. *Everyone's* going to be there."

She groaned, a low, painful sound she didn't tell her body to make. "What if I mess up? I haven't been on live TV for a long time."

"Everyone here loves you, and everyone in Corpus Christi loves you." He kissed her cheek, the corner of her mouth, the crook of her neck. "I love you. No one's going to care if you mess up. Plus." He pulled back and grinned down at her. "It might be nice to see you do something less than perfect."

She swatted at his arms, but he held her fast. "I am not perfect at everything I do."

"Have you seen my cabin after you clean it? Have you tasted your own cooking?"

She cocked her head at him. "Am I really that good of a cook?"

"Phenomenal." He leaned down to kiss her, but she jerked back. He peered at her, waiting for her to explain herself.

"Could I get a job as a cook in town, do you think?"

"Taryn, I think you could do whatever you want to do." He gazed at her with such love and adoration, warmth flowed through her like a bubbling hot spring.

"Kenny, I have a Christmas gift for you."

His smile was wide and instant. "Oh, yeah? I have something for you too."

"Can we exchange on Christmas morning?" She hoped she wouldn't lose her courage over the next couple of days.

"Of course."

"I managed to get an apple pie from Grace Lewis, and I think I'll make a ham. Is that what you had for your family Christmas dinners?"

"My mom's not much of a cook."

Taryn laughed. "No wonder you think I'm a good cook." She stepped out of his arms, a bit surprised that he let her. "Maybe I won't be able to get a job in a restaurant."

"Sure you will. Like I said, you can do anything you want to do."

* * *

By the following evening, Taryn could barely remember Kenny's reassurances. They'd gotten her through filling out a half dozen applications that morning. His vote of confidence had helped her finish her preparations for the op-ed piece. The camera crew had arrived two hours ago, and she'd walked them through what she wanted, where she'd move, when they should pan out, and when they should voice over.

The sun had started to set, and the Christmas lights on Main Street gave such warmth to the town that Taryn knew why she'd chosen to stay here.

She tugged at the hem of her new peacoat, another purchase from Andy Larsen, the boutique owner who Taryn needed to become besties with to start saving on her purchases. She fiddled with her ear mic, the way she used to before a broadcast.

Stanley had sent a crew of five for her special. He himself hadn't come, something for which she was grateful. She didn't recognize any of the cameramen either, though they all seemed to know who she was.

The seconds blurred into minutes, and then one of the men said, "And you're live in five, four...." He held up three fingers, two, then one, and Taryn took a deep breath.

"I'm Taryn Tucker, on location here in beautiful, festive, Three Rivers, Texas. This small town has big charm, as you can see from the holiday excitement behind me." She turned, caught a glimpse of Kenny's beaming face, and knew that everything was going to turn out all right.

* * *

Kenny watched as Taryn oozed charisma, as she chatted with townspeople, as she charmed everyone in Three Rivers, the camera, and anyone on the other end of the feed. No wonder she'd been popular in Corpus Christi.

He'd gone online—probably a mistake—and seen dozens of open letters to "Miss Taryn Tucker, the heart of Corpus Christi" on forums and blogs. She'd had a real following. Part of him couldn't believe that she could just walk away from all of that. Another part of him admired her for doing it. A third part wondered if she ever missed being on-camera.

And now, watching her, he knew she did. He also believed she truly didn't want to return to that life. He didn't want her to either. He wanted to keep her as close as possible until the day he could ask her to be his wife.

He drifted away from the scene as she wrapped up the segment. She'd seemed nervous that he'd be there, and he'd tried to stay near the back of the crowd. They were meeting at the pancake house for celebratory hot chocolates, and Kenny wandered in that direction.

Several cowhands from the ranch passed by, each inviting him to join them for the evening. The owner,

Squire Ackerman, caught his eye and Kenny stopped to chat for a second.

"You alone?" Squire asked, his right hand holding his wife's and his left clutching Finn's. Another little girl clung to Kelly's shoulder as she balanced her on her hip.

"On my way to meet someone."

"Taryn," Kelly said with a knowing smile. "I know everything that happens out on my ranch."

Kenny's heart skipped a beat as Squire turned toward Kelly with an arched brow. "*Your* ranch? And what do we feed the cattle?"

She nudged him with her shoulder. "Fine, I know everything that happens to the people out on *our* ranch." She slid a mischievous glance at Kenny. "Including where and with whom they eat lunch."

Kenny's face heated, and he tipped his hat to her. "It's no secret I'm datin' Taryn."

"It isn't?" Squire whipped his face back to Kenny's.

Kelly laughed. "Squire, I swear. You're the last to know everything that happens. Even Pete knew."

"Well, Taryn is his client," Kenny said quickly. "Don't feel too bad, Major."

Squire gazed toward the hullaballoo down the block. "She's not gonna stay on much longer, is she?" He wasn't really asking, and Kenny chuckled.

"My guess is no," he said. "Which is a real shame, because I've sure enjoyed her housekeeping."

"Well, you'll just have to marry her," Kelly singsonged.

Kenny's joy tumbled down a notch. "We're in negotiations."

"Negotiations?" Squire burst out laughing. "Women don't like military talk."

Kenny grinned at him. "She's...working through a few things before we get serious enough to be talkin' diamonds."

"And you?" he asked. "You have anything to work through?"

"Just how to keep her happy until she realizes I'm her one and only." Kenny lowered his voice. "And I'd appreciate it if that stayed between me and you, Miss Kelly."

"Of course."

"At least he knows who the gossipy one is," Squire said.

"I am not gossipy." She hipped Squire this time. "But I probably will tell Chelsea."

"Shouldn't have said anything," Squire said as he started walking away. "Once my sister knows, the whole county will know."

"No problem," Kenny called after them, but a jiggle of anxiety wormed through his bloodstream.

* * *

On Christmas Day, Kenny arrived at Taryn's about mid-morning. She wore her hair up in a messy bun, revealing her very kissable neck, and a festive red and white sweater dress that hugged every curve.

Kenny swallowed as he entered her apartment and she locked them in together. "Have you ever had funeral potatoes?"

"Yeah, sure, every time someone dies." He followed her into the kitchen. "Is that what you're making? Because I've never met a potato I didn't like."

She giggled. "You'll eat anything. I could put butter on a brick and you'd tell me it was the best sandwich you've ever had."

"That is so not true."

She cocked her hip and he lunged toward her, catching her up and twirling her around. She squealed and grabbed onto his shoulders. He loved the way she made him feel: powerful and strong and necessary. He loved being with her. He loved that he could offer her shelter from the storms of life. He loved her.

"Let's do gifts now," he said, setting her on her feet.

A blip of panic stole across her face. "Now?"

He pulled out the envelope he'd put her tickets in. "Yeah, now." He held his gift toward her. She took it and retrieved a small, silver box from the top of her fridge. Bigger than a ring box, but it probably couldn't hold more than a can of soda.

She slipped her finger under the envelope's flap and extracted the tickets. "Kitty Hawk...Kenny. What is this?"

"You said you love to travel, but that you didn't get to do much of it for pleasure. I thought, well, I thought we could take a vacation—a real vacation together. They're vouchers, good for up to twenty-four months. So, you know, you don't have to decide right away or anything."

She held them to her heartbeat like they were precious, made of gold. Her eyes seemed a bit glassy when she said, "Thank you, Kenny," and stretched up to kiss him. He enjoyed the feel and form of her lips against his. She was all he needed for Christmas.

But she pulled away and thrust the silver box toward him. He took it and lifted the lid. Beneath a slip of white tissue paper sat a gold key. A regular, shiny, gold key, like he would use to secure the deadbolt on his cabin.

He glanced at her, unsure about what this key unlocked. "Taryn?"

Her hands wrung around each other. "That's the key to my new house. I picked it up last Friday, and I'm moving in a couple of days." She swallowed, that hard, nervous swallow he wanted to eradicate from her life.

"I wanted you to have a key, because it represents how I feel about Three Rivers, how I feel about us."

He flipped the key in his fingers, his eyes trained on the shiny metal. "You're stayin' here permanently." Joy he'd never known spiraled through his chest.

"I am. My new house is in that Pinion Ridge development."

Kenny nodded, and his head felt too loose, almost detached from his shoulders. "That's great news." He finally lifted his eyes to hers. "I love you."

She invaded his personal space, pressing herself as close to him as she could get. "In this moment, I love you too."

It wasn't the all-out declaration Kenny craved, but in this moment, he'd take it. Because he knew she was dangerously close to being able to tell him she loved him all the time.

* * *

THE NEXT CHRISTMAS:

"Where's Taryn?" Pete entered the homestead, along with a heavy gust of wind. Kenny's already keyed-up nerves rioted again.

"She's comin'." He wished he hadn't told Charlie about his forthcoming proposal. The news had spread like wildfire, and it was all anyone had talked about for weeks. Even when Taryn came out for her riding lessons or just to see him. It was nothing short of a miracle that she hadn't overheard, that she didn't know.

Maybe she did.

Kenny's stomach swooped as the door opened again, but this time Garth and Juliette ducked into the house with their son right in front of them.

"Did we miss it?" Garth asked, glancing around at everyone in the kitchen, dining room, and living area of Squire's house. Kelly had gone all out for this holiday season. She'd had plenty of help from Chelsea and Heidi. Grace Lewis, the best pastry chef Three Rivers had ever seen, busied herself at the stove, stirring something that normally would've made Kenny double-sniff the air and become impatient for dessert later.

Squire consulted with Jon Carver and Lawrence about how to carve the turkeys, while Lawrence's wife, Andy, kept one hand on her bulging belly while she spoke to Sandy Keller, who'd just been the star of autumn with her wedding to Tad Jorgensen.

Bees buzzed in Kenny's blood. Snakes coiled in his gut. What had he been thinking? Taryn wouldn't want her engagement to be a public spectacle. Maybe it wasn't too late to call everything off. He opened his mouth to say something when the door opened again.

"Sorry I'm late." The wind caught the door behind Taryn, but she won the struggle and yanked it closed.

"Phew, it's really angry out there." She smiled at Kenny and stepped to his side, her arm sliding around his waist. "Hey."

He pressed a nervous kiss to her temple and glanced around. It seemed like everyone had at least one eye on him, and he focused his attention back on Taryn. "Everything go okay getting the recording off?"

She'd taken a remote job with her old station, and she did three yearly holiday specials. One always fell on Christmas Eve, which she'd just finished the previous evening.

"All set. What did I miss here?"

"Just Ethan braggin' about how he won Rookie of the Year," Garth said. He lifted a mug of coffee to hide his obviously proud smile. "*Last* year."

"Hey," Ethan complained. "I wasn't bragging. Brynn was bragging for me." He beamed down at his fiancé.

"When are y'all getting married?" Carly Sanders joined their conversation as she bounced a beautiful baby boy on her hip. Kenny watched the child smile and slobber, and warmth filled his heart.

"Next month." Brynn glanced at him with love but a touch of wistfulness. "Your baby is so cute," she told Carly.

Reese slid next to her, and together, they made a beautiful family. It didn't matter that their baby wasn't theirs biologically. He belonged to them, and they adored him. Kenny kneaded Taryn a tiny bit closer.

"We ready to eat yet?" Frank Ackerman appeared at the mouth of the hallway, forever wearing his cowboy hat and boots. He'd hired Kenny five years ago, and Kenny still felt a flash of appreciation whenever he saw the man.

"Brett and Kate aren't here yet," Squire said. "They're bringin' the rolls from the bakery."

"See? You weren't last." Kenny smiled at Taryn, who returned the gesture. All his nerves settled. He loved her, and she loved him, and he didn't doubt for a moment that she'd say yes to his very important question.

He retreated a few steps as he watched the people around him. The foreman he appreciated and obeyed. The men who'd gone off to war, come home broken, and found a way to make a life for themselves at Three Rivers Ranch.

The rodeo champions, and the horse boarders, and the pancake house owners. Kenny felt such love for them all, he thought sure his heart would burst.

Brett and Kate arrived a few minutes later, towing their two kids and dozens and dozens of rolls with them.

"All right," Squire said, sending Kenny's pulse into a tizzy. "We're all here now."

"'Cept Tom," Pete said.

"Of course. Except Tom." A moment passed in silence while Kenny pictured the steady, sure cowboy who'd been the controller on the ranch. He'd been gone for a couple of years, but he came back to visit from time to time. He'd been here over the Fourth of July, but wanted to build his own family holiday traditions on the ranch where he now lived in Montana.

"I just want to say how grateful I am for all of you." Squire swallowed, the only emotion he ever showed. "And for God for bringin' you all out to Three Rivers, in whatever way He did." He lifted his mug; Pete whooped; everyone broke into applause.

"And now, I believe we have a program of sorts that's been prepared." Squire's gaze landed on Kenny. Everyone's did. Garth slid the jewelry box into Kenny's hand, but he couldn't seem to move.

"Go on, now." Pete looked like the cat who'd swallowed the canary.

"Kenny—" Taryn started as she glanced around at the obvious audience.

"Taryn." He turned toward her. "I've loved you since last Christmas, when you became the best present I'd ever gotten. Will you do me one better this year by agreein' to be my wife?" He dropped to one knee, but with his height, he barely had to look up into her face.

A single tear slithered down her right cheek. She nodded.

"Make her say yes!" someone called.

"Taryn?" Kenny grinned at her. "You better say yes for the people."

"Yes."

He swooped her into his arms and kissed her. "Best Christmas ever," he whispered as he set her down and rested his forehead against hers. "I love you."

"I love you, too, Kenny."

"Let's eat," Frank said, and the chaos Kenny was used to—the business and liveliness of the ranch he loved—ensued. He felt like the luckiest man in the world, and he closed his eyes and sent a prayer of thanksgiving toward heaven to be here, in Three Rivers, on the ranch, with the people he loved most.

Especially Taryn, he thought just before opening his eyes to the spread of what was sure to be the most delicious Christmas feast he'd ever eaten.

Get ready for more cowboy romance at Three Rivers Ranch! **Read on for a sneak peek at LUCKY NUMBER THIRTEEN,** the next book in the Three Rivers Ranch Romance™ series!

Sneak Peek! Lucky Number Thirteen Chapter One

"Tanner!"

Tanner Wolf turned at the sound of his name in a female voice. A blond man strode toward him, his hand secured in a dark haired woman's.

A smile warmed his soul. "Brynn."

She laughed as he embraced her, and Ethan's grin seemed as wide as the sky over Montana. "Hey, Tanner." He slapped Tanner on the back. "That was some impressive roping."

"Thanks." He brushed some invisible dust from his hands and a lot of very visible dirt from his chaps. "Nothin' like me and you, but Dallas does all right."

"All right?" Brynn scoffed. "You'll take first with that, and from what I hear, you guys won't be beat this year."

Tanner tried to shrug off their compliments. Since

Ethan had chosen Brynn over rodeo, chosen Three Rivers over Colorado, chosen his faith over everything, Tanner had searched his soul. It wasn't easy, and he'd found a lot of darkness inside. He still wasn't all the way where he wanted to be, and being humble didn't come naturally to him.

After all, he'd spent the last thirty years of his life trying to be the best and celebrating when he was.

"You're comin' out to the ranch for the picnic, right?" Ethan asked. Tanner had been in touch with him over the past couple of years, and when his manager had added the Three Rivers rodeo to his schedule, Tanner had called Ethan first.

"Yeah, of course. Tomorrow at four. I've been to the ranch before."

"You haven't seen my training facilities," Brynn said as a group of cowgirls walked by. Her gaze followed them, and Tanner wondered if she missed the rodeo circuit. She'd quit and never looked back, but a glint rode in her eye that Tanner recognized.

"I'll come early," Tanner said. "Will you guys be out there?"

"We can go out whenever we want," Brynn said.

"I want to see your place too," Tanner said. "Ethan's been bragging about how he built it from the ground up."

"I haven't been bragging."

103

"I believe you said, 'with my bare hands, Tanner. I built a whole house with my bare hands.'"

Ethan chuckled, and a wave a gratitude washed over Tanner. He couldn't believe Ethan's forgiveness had come so quickly, had healed him so completely. But it had done both, and though he'd never told Ethan, it was his forgiveness that had set Tanner down the path toward a relationship with God.

Of course, that had meant his relationships with women had cooled considerably as he navigated his way toward becoming the kind of man he wanted to be. In fact, his last date had been over a year ago, and that relationship had fizzled before the end of the evening.

"Mister Wolf, you're up in twenty," a rodeo volunteer said, stepping into their conversation.

Tanner took a deep breath, his nerves blossoming into a hill of ants. "All right, wish me luck."

"Who'd you draw?" Ethan asked.

"Lucky Number Thirteen," Tanner said, his voice a note higher than normal. "I've never ridden him to the bell."

Brynn's dark eyes caught on his and her hand landed on his forearm. "You'll get 'im this time." She added a smile to her statement, and Tanner couldn't detect a hint of falseness in her voice.

He managed to smile, mash his cowboy hat further

down on his head, and follow the volunteer to the loading chutes.

He'd ridden hundreds of bulls over his twelve-year career. He'd drawn easy wins and nasty animals. He'd never had a bull he hadn't been able to ride. Eventually, they all succumbed to Tanner and the eight-second bell.

He eyed Lucky Number Thirteen, the black and white bull he'd come up against in San Antonio earlier this year. He'd only made it three seconds on the animal, and that disastrous ride played through his mind as the other riders took their turns.

Finally, he sat in the saddle. He pulled the rope across his palm tight, tight. He drew breath after breath to calm his heart, relax his muscles. None of the calming techniques worked, and he had a brief second to wonder if he should've asked for a helmet before the bell rang and the gate opened.

The crowd blurred as it always did while he rode. He only felt the bull's muscles beneath his body. Only listened for the alarm signaling he'd made it to eight seconds. Only breathed once the ride ended.

Lucky Number Thirteen reared, driving right back into Tanner's chest. He slipped, and he knew he was going off despite his strong muscles and iron will trying to hold him on the bull's back.

His feet didn't hit the dirt first; his back did. Hard.

The air in his lungs seized, and he couldn't take another breath. The bright lights in the arena went dark as the bull kicked, loomed above him, and all Tanner saw was dark sky and dark animal flesh, and a horrifying dark hoof as it crashed into his ribs.

He instinctively curled into himself, protecting his most vital organs. Around him, he heard shouts, silence, the announcers, the snuffling of the bull, the call of the clowns. He couldn't breathe, couldn't breathe, and pressed his chin to his chest and kept his elbows up as another lightning hot pain shot through his back, down into both his legs.

Time seemed to slow and everything felt shrouded in darkness.

Finally, everything brightened again, and Tanner relaxed. His brain seemed to be working just fine, but every cell in his body screamed in pain. He groaned as he started to uncurl.

"Don't move," someone said, his hand landing lightly on Tanner's forehead. He said something else, his gaze darting away, but Tanner closed his eyes and focused on breathing. Breathing was good. Breathing was necessary.

Movement happened around him. Men spoke in calm voices. Tanner felt the summer air turn cold as something pooled beneath his head. He tried to reach for it, but someone stopped him.

"Lie still, Tanner." A familiar face, with bright green eyes and that shock of blond hair, filled his vision.

"Ethan," Tanner moaned. *Help me,* he prayed, and though he was new to the whole communicating with God idea, the thought felt natural.

"You're fine, cowboy." Ethan's eyes said otherwise, and Tanner tried to focus on them. But they turned lighter and lighter, going into seafoam and mint before they faded into whiteness.

"Stay with me," Ethan commanded, but Tanner couldn't. He closed his eyes against the pain and let unconsciousness take him somewhere where he wasn't lying in his own blood in the middle of the rodeo arena.

* * *

WHEN HE WOKE, a pair of eyes the color of the ocean blinked at him. "There you are, Mister Wolf." The woman spoke in a slow cadence, her accent Texan and sweet. She glanced down at his chart, wrote something, and looked at him again. "How are you feeling?"

He couldn't vocalize the words he used to, and his back and arm muscles seemed to have forgotten how to shrug.

"My name's Summer, and I'll be your nurse today.

Now Jean said you slept all night, and came through your surgery just fine."

He blinked at her, a searing pain in his throat. He could only think, *Surgery?*

"Now, you'll have to get up in a few hours and take a walk around." She grinned at him, and he thought she had the most wonderful pink lips, the most beautiful white teeth. His first instinct was to smile back, and he tried, but something seemed to be wrong with his mouth.

"I don't want any complaints when I come back," she said, her eyes dipping to his lips. "I'll go get Margie, and we'll get that tube out of your throat." She disappeared from his line of sight, and Tanner found pain in every part of his body. How Summer thought he could answer her questions with a tube down his throat, he didn't know.

She returned lickety split, and before he knew it, the two nurses had removed the tube from his throat.

"He's making urine," the other nurse said. She beamed at him, and he'd never been prouder of his body for functioning the way it should. She was closer to his mother's age, and panic pounded through him.

"My...mom?" His throat hurt, and Summer was there, holding out a glass of water. He gulped it greedily as Margie explained that she'd been notified and that she should be here soon.

"There's a couple of friends out in the waiting room," she said. "Should I send them in?"

"How much pain are you in?" Summer asked before Tanner could answer Margie.

"Is 'about to die' on your chart?" he croaked.

She grinned. "Yes, we call that a ten. I'll bring you something."

"A lot of something," he said as a pain in his leg fired on all cylinders. "Something strong."

Margie met Summer's eye and the two nurses exchanged a glance. "Something strong, Mister Wolf," Summer said, her voice full of fun and flirtation.

Tanner sat back in bed as they left, warning himself to maintain distance from Summer. He didn't live in Three Rivers, and she'd go home—maybe to a husband and a family—later that day.

She sure is pretty though, he thought as he waited for his medicine and his friends. The friends came first, and Ethan and Brynn looked like they hadn't gone home to sleep.

Tears tracked down Brynn's cheeks as she leaned over and gave Tanner a light hug. He couldn't help the groan of pain from the movement and she jerked back. "Sorry."

"I'm fine." He pushed himself up in bed, a flash of discomfort spreading through his right leg. "Aren't I fine, Ethan?"

He watched his friend for the signs he needed. Ethan kept his face a blank slate, but the intensity of his swallow told Tanner everything.

"Yeah," Ethan said. "You're going to be just fine, Tanner."

Tanner looked away as emotion surged up his throat. He knew by Ethan's reaction that he'd never ride bulls again.

With that swallow, Tanner knew his rodeo career had ended, right there in the Three Rivers arena.

* * *

A rodeo star, a nurse, and a summer to remember...
Read LUCKY NUMBER THIRTEEN now!
Scan the QR code below to look for it.

Second Chance Ranch: A Three Rivers Ranch Romance™ (Book 1): After his deployment, injured and discharged Major Squire Ackerman returns to Three Rivers Ranch, wanting to forgive Kelly for ignoring him a decade ago. He'd like to provide the stable life she needs, but with old wounds opening and a ranch on the brink of financial collapse, it will take patience and faith to make their second chance possible.

Third Time's the Charm: A Three Rivers Ranch Romance™ (Book 2): First Lieutenant Peter Marshall has a truck-load of debt and no way to provide for a family, but Chelsea helps him see past all the obstacles, all the scars. With so many unknowns, can Pete and Chelsea develop the love, acceptance, and faith needed to find their happily ever after?

Fourth and Long: A Three Rivers Ranch Romance™ (Book 3): Commander Brett Murphy goes to Three Rivers Ranch to find some rest and relaxation with his Army buddies. Having his ex-wife show up with a seven-year-old she claims is his son is anything but the R&R he craves. Kate needs to make amends, and Brett needs to find forgiveness, but are they too late to find their happily ever after?

Fifth Generation Cowboy: A Three Rivers Ranch Romance™ (Book 4): Tom Lovell has watched his friends find their true happiness on Three Rivers Ranch, but everywhere he looks, he only sees friends. Rose Reyes has been bringing her daughter out to the ranch for equine therapy for months, but it doesn't seem to be working. Her challenges with Mari are just as frustrating as ever. Could Tom be exactly what Rose needs? Can he remove his friendship blinders and find love with someone who's been right in front of him all this time?

Sixth Street Love Affair: A Three Rivers Ranch Romance™ (Book 5): After losing his wife a few years back, Garth Ahlstrom thinks he's ready for a second chance at love. But Juliette Thompson has a secret that could destroy their budding relationship. Can they find the strength, patience, and faith to make things work?

The Seventh Sergeant: A Three Rivers Ranch Romance™ (Book 6): Life has finally started to settle down for Sergeant Reese Sanders after his devastating injury overseas. Discharged from the Army and now with a good job at Courage Reins, he's finally found happiness—until a horrific fall puts him right back where he was years ago: Injured and depressed. Carly Watters, Reese's new veteran care coordinator, dislikes small towns almost as much as she loathes cowboys. But she finds herself faced with both when she gets assigned to Reese's case. Do they have the humility and faith to make their relationship more than professional?

Eight Second Ride: A Three Rivers Ranch Romance™ (Book 7): Ethan Greene loves his work at Three Rivers Ranch, but he can't seem to find the right woman to settle down with. When sassy yet vulnerable Brynn Bowman shows up at the ranch to recruit him back to the rodeo circuit, he takes a different approach with the barrel racing champion. His patience and newfound faith pay off when a friendship--and more--starts with Brynn. But she wants out of the rodeo circuit right when Ethan wants to rejoin. Can they find the path God wants them to take and still stay together?

The Ninth Inning: A Three Rivers Ranch Romance™ (Book 8): The Christmas season has never felt like such a burden to boutique owner Andrea Larsen. But with Mama gone and the holidays upon her, Andy finds herself wishing she hadn't been so quick to judge her former boyfriend, cowboy Lawrence Collins. Well, Lawrence hasn't forgotten about Andy either, and he devises a plan to get her out to the ranch so they can reconnect. Do they have the faith and humility to patch things up and start a new relationship?

Ten Days in Town: A Three Rivers Ranch Romance™ (Book 9): Sandy Keller is tired of the dating scene in Three Rivers. Though she owns the pancake house, she's looking for a fresh start, which means an escape from the town where she grew up. When her older brother's best friend, Tad Jorgensen, comes to town for the holidays, it is a balm to his weary soul. A helicopter tour guide who experienced a near-death experience, he's looking to start over too--but in Three Rivers. Can Sandy and Tad navigate their troubles to find the path God wants them to take--and discover true love--in only ten days?

Eleven Year Reunion: A Three Rivers Ranch Romance™ (Book 10): Pastry chef extraordinaire, Grace Lewis has moved to Three Rivers to help Heidi Ackerman open a bakery in Three Rivers. Grace relishes the idea of starting over in a town where no one knows about her failed cupcakery. She doesn't expect to run into her old high school boyfriend, Jonathan Carver. A carpenter working at Three Rivers Ranch, Jon's in town against his will. But with Grace now on the scene, Jon's thinking life in Three Rivers is suddenly looking up. But with her focus on baking and his disdain for small towns, can they make their eleven year reunion stick?

The Twelfth Town: A Three Rivers Ranch Romance™ (Book 11): Newscaster Taryn Tucker has had enough of life on-screen. She's bounced from town to town before arriving in Three Rivers, completely alone and completely anony-mous--just the way she now likes it. She takes a job cleaning at Three Rivers Ranch, hoping for a chance to figure out who she is and where God wants her. When she meets happy-go-lucky cowhand Kenny Stockton, she doesn't expect sparks to fly. Kenny's always been "the best friend" for his female friends, but the pull between him and Taryn can't be denied. Will they have the courage and faith necessary to make their opposite worlds mesh?

Lucky Number Thirteen: A Three Rivers Ranch Romance™ (Book 12): Tanner Wolf, a rodeo champion ten times over, is excited to be riding in Three Rivers for the first time since he left his philandering ways and found religion. Seeing his old friends Ethan and Brynn is therapuetic--until a terrible accident lands him in the hospital. With his rodeo career over, Tanner thinks maybe he'll stay in town--and it's not just because his nurse, Summer Hamblin, is the prettiest woman he's ever met. But Summer's the queen of first dates, and as she looks for a way to make a relationship with the transient rodeo star work Summer's not sure she has the fortitude to go on a second date. Can they find love among the tragedy?

The Curse of February Fourteenth: A Three Rivers Ranch Romance™ (Book 13): Cal Hodgkins, cowboy veterinarian at Bowman's Breeds, isn't planning to meet anyone at the masked dance in small-town Three Rivers. He just wants to get his bachelor friends off his back and sit on the sidelines to drink his punch. But when he sees a woman dressed in gorgeous butterfly wings and cowgirl boots with blue stitching, he's smitten. Too bad she runs away from the dance before he can get her name, leaving only her boot behind...

Fifteen Minutes of Fame: A Three Rivers Ranch Romance™ (Book 14): Navy Richards is thirty-five years of tired— tired of dating the same men, working a demanding job, and getting her heart broken over and over again. Her aunt has always spoken highly of the matchmaker in Three Rivers, Texas, so she takes a six-month sabbatical from her high-stress job as a pediatric nurse, hops on a bus, and meets with the matchmaker. Then she meets Gavin Redd. He's handsome, he's hardworking, and he's a cowboy. But is he an Aquarius too? Navy's not making a move until she knows for sure...

Sixteen Steps to Fall in Love: A Three Rivers Ranch Romance™ (Book 15): A chance encounter at a dog park sheds new light on the tall, talented Boone that Nicole can't ignore. As they get to know each other better and start to dig into each other's past, Nicole is the one who wants to run. This time from her growing admiration and attachment to Boone. From her aging parents. From herself.

But Boone feels the attraction between them too, and he decides he's tired of running and ready to make Three Rivers his permanent home. **Can Boone and Nicole use their faith to overcome their differences and find a happily-ever-after together?**

The Sleigh on Seventeenth Street: A Three Rivers Ranch Romance™ (Book 16): A cowboy with skills as an electrician tries a relationship with a down-on-her luck plumber. Can Dylan and Camila make water and electricity play nicely together this Christmas season? Or will they get shocked as they try to make their relationship work?

The First Lady of Three Rivers Ranch: A Three Rivers Ranch Romance™ (Book 17): Heidi Duffin has been dreaming about opening her own bakery since she was thirteen years old. She scrimped and saved for years to afford baking and pastry school in San Francisco. And now she only has one year left before she's a certified pastry chef. Frank Ackerman's father has recently retired, and he's taken over the largest cattle ranch in the Texas Panhandle. A horseman through and through, he's also nearing thirty-one and looking for someone to bring love and joy to a homestead that's been dominated by men for a decade. But when he convinces Heidi to come clean the cowboy cabins, she changes all that. But the siren's call of a bakery is still loud in Heidi's ears, even if she's also seeing a future with Frank. Can she rely on her faith in ways she's never had to before or will their relationship end when summer does?

Second Generation in Three Rivers Romance™ Series

Step back into the heartwarming small Texas town of Three Rivers! This beloved town has captured the hearts of 2.5 million readers and caught the eye of Sony Pictures, and now a new generation of cowboys and cowgirls is ready to take center stage. Scan the QR code below with your phone to check out this new series!

1. The Cowboy Who Came Home - featuring Squire's son, Finn from SECOND CHANCE RANCH!

Seven Sons Ranch in Three Rivers Romance™ Series

Meet the cowboy billionaire brothers at Seven Sons Ranch! Scan the QR code below with your phone to check out this complete series.

Shiloh Ridge Ranch in Three Rivers Romance™ Series

Meet the cowboy billionaires in the southern hills outside of Three Rivers! Scan the QR code below with your phone to check out this complete series.

About Liz

Liz Isaacson writes inspirational romance, usually set in Texas, or Wyoming, or anywhere else horses and cowboys exist. She lives in Utah, where she writes full-time, takes her two dogs to the park everyday, and eats a lot of veggies while writing. Find all of her books on her website at feelgoodfictionbooks.com.